# SPACE COFFIN

The old man on the stretcher senses his impending death and struggles to regain unconsciousness. Van Buren's eyes have a drugged look as he pulls the lever protruding from the air lock. Silently the stretcher is wheeled into the chamber. As the air from the compartment escapes, the body starts to quiver slightly. The cheeks sink in, giving the face the appearance of a skull. On the dead man's lips, bubbles form, grow, burst, and evaporate as if the corpse were boiling inside. Not wanting to upset his appetite, Van Buren walks away, every step covering ten feet of space in the reduced gravity of the Space Prison.

It was a hell of a way to vacate a room.

# City in the Sky

CURT SIODMAK

PINNACLE BOOKS • NEW YORK CITY

This is a work of fiction. All the characters and events portrayed in this book are fictional, and any resemblance to real people or incidents is purely coincidental.

CITY IN THE SKY



A Pinnacle Books edition, published by special arrangement with G. P. Putnam's Sons

ISBN: 0-523-00582-2

First printing, April 1975

*Printed in the United States of America*

PINNACLE BOOKS, INC.
275 Madison Avenue
New York, N.Y. 10016

FOR GEOFFREY AND DOREEN
AND CAROL AND LYNN

# I

Jan Van Buren's angelic face bends over the old man on the narrow bed in the Space Prison. His deepset eyes, glittering and soulless as if cut from crystal, watch with sensual pleasure the drugged man's agony.

Through the Vycor glass of the room the earth leaps like a giant, filling star-studded space, disappearing as the satellite turns on its axis.

Van Buren straightens his carefully exercised frame narcissistically, shaking his shoulder-length blond hair.

"He starts fighting the drug," he says to Hans Hallstadt, pronouncing every syllable with elocutionary care. "Let's get through with it before he wakes up."

The room is almost bare, except for a table fastened to the floor, a chair swinging cantilevered from the wall, a bookshelf holding a few volumes, clamped together to prevent them from floating in the satellite's reduced gravity.

"This is a hell of a way to vacate a room!" Hallstadt remarks. His face, blotched by the cancer which a tropical sun has burned into his skin, grins sadly, conveying compassion.

Van Buren lifts the old man and slides him onto a stretcher with Hallstadt's help.

"He doesn't know," Van Buren says to console Hallstadt. A chemistry exists between the two men that surpasses friendship.

"He's known it for some time," Hallstadt says with a concern which does not seem to pertain to the drugged man, but to himself. "He still had a few years in him."

They lift the stretcher. In the reduced gravity it seems almost weightless.

"He doesn't know!" Van Buren repeats with fierce impatience. "And if he did, he didn't know when. So what? It's like being hit by a stroke. Suddenly. Unexpectedly. Do you want to know when you're going to die?"

"They won't kill me that way!" Hallstadt mutters.

They enter a corridor and walk past closed doors.

"Ground is sending up a replacement. Pierre Bardou, a Frenchman," Hallstadt says. He carries the stretcher like a waiter with a tray.

"What's his crime?" Van Buren asks with flat sarcasm. "Did he try to assassinate the French President?"

"No. He published secret papers that exposed the French military."

"Ah! Attacking the military! That's a crime worse than murder!" Van Buren stops, putting down the stretcher. "First comes God, then the generals, or vice versa!"

"War is an exciting profession," Hallstadt says. "You ought to know. You like to see people die."

They have reached a small cove in the corridor's wall. A heavy door, half round, with a heavy steel frame like those in submarines, closes an air lock which leads to outer space. The old man on the stretcher senses his impending death and struggles to regain consciousness. He chatters broken sentences. Hallstadt bends over him, but Van Buren pulls back gently.

"Don't listen, Hans." Van Buren's eyes have a drugged, occult look. "Those words mean nothing, but they will stay with you."

He pulls a lever protruding from the wall; air hisses like an animal's voice from behind the door. Van Buren watches gauges which measure the air pressure inside the air lock. The atmospheres equalize, and the door slowly swings open.

"You don't need to stay around, Hans. I know you have a soft kernel in your rotten soul," Van Buren says, breathing fast, touching his friend's face with a fleeting gesture.

"I don't mind," Hallstadt says with a shrug. "How many have we shoved in here? It's no great discomfort to *me*."

Silently the two men wheel the stretcher into the air lock, then close the heavy door.

"I've listened to Bardou's trial on video," Hallstadt says, watching Van Buren pull the lever down. The staccato rhythm of the compressor whirls. "He almost got himself acquitted, but then there was some shooting outside the courtroom, and people got killed. That's why the judge sent him up to us."

"Mysterious!" Van Buren puts his palms against the Vycor glass and stares down at the figure on the stretcher. "Pressure equalized," he mutters. "Open the outer door."

Air from the lock streams back into the pressure drums. A wall in the air lock slides open, and black space shining with galaxies forms a velvety backdrop.

"Not mysterious at all," Hallstadt says, continuing the conversation. He rolls a cigarette, lights it and inhales deeply. Then he passes the cigarette to his friend, who is engrossed in observing the man in the air lock; he takes it from Hallstadt without turning his head. "Governments never give up when they're after their prey," Hallstadt says. "Never! Bardou didn't have a chance!"

The body in the air lock lies perfectly still. But now it starts to quiver slightly, almost imperceptibly. The cheeks sink in, giving the face the appearance of a skull. The eyes drop back into their sockets, and the skin starts to shrink, pushing out gray stubbles of hair. Van Buren watches the transformation with hypnotic concentration.

"I can't see that often enough," he confesses without apology. "Watching people die this way makes me philosophical. What are we? Ninety-five percent water and a few pounds of bones, hair, flesh and nails? How can man be the image of God? Is God made of water?" He chuckles.

Bubbles form on the dead man's lips, grow, burst and evaporate, as if the corpse were boiling inside. His clothing, a gown like those which Hallstadt and Van Buren are wearing, becomes too large for his frame.

"Leave him alone." Hallstadt turns his face away, tugs his friend's arm. "It takes hours before he desiccates. It isn't a pleasant sight, just before dinner."

Taking the cigarette from Van Buren's lips, he inhales deeply.

Van Buren cannot take his eyes from the shrinking body. "I love to watch. Do you think Bardou will fit our little community?"

"He might. He sounds intelligent," Hallstadt says. "And if he doesn't, we'll have an empty room, but not for long. They have them piled up down there, I understand. Ground is happy about anybody up here dying. If they could find a way, they'd rotate the whole crew every month!"

He glances at the body. It has changed shape. The legs lift up slowly as though pulled by strings. The skin has turned to parchment. Van Buren presses his face hard against the glass.

"Have fun, you sadistic son of a bitch." Hallstadt slaps Van Buren's back playfully. "What a way to get your sex kicks! Somebody has to die for you to get an orgasm!"

Van Buren pays no attention to him. Hallstadt with storklike movements walks away, every step covering ten feet of space in the reduced gravity of the Space Prison.

# II

Lee Powers is talking to Evgeny Rubikov on the videophone which connects his chalet in the Swiss town of Thun with the International Space City. Rubikov looks wan and nervous on the small television screen—Rubikov, who boasts that he is able to "fly into a terrific calm" whenever a situation becomes critical.

"You'd better come up with the next shuttle," Rubikov barks. "Damn it, you're the captain of this contraption; your job is up here. Stop going fishing. I refuse to take on added responsibilities!"

"What's up, Ev?" Lee asks. "Got a dose of astrophobia?"

Rubikov does not respond to his joke except to become even more intense.

"We've got a radioactive leak in or around Reactor One. I've sealed off the globe and switched the power to number three. Two is inoperative; its fuel is being changed. If something happens to number three, we have no power at all and the ISC will freeze up in two days!"

There are nearly three thousand people in the International Space City.

"Just calm down, Ev. Reactor Two can always be made operative in a few hours."

Lee is fighting with the board of directors of the International Space City to add another reactor to the ISC. Will it require a disaster of major proportions before he can pry loose the finances from the board?

"If the leak is in the boiler-turbo machinery, we have a chance to patch it up. If it is in Reactor One, we'll have to dismantle it and ship it back to earth. We couldn't repair it up here!" Rubikov says with unnatural calm. "I started draining the sodium potassium into containers to get my crew to the leak area. I've called already for space tugs to carry all that junk out of here, just in case. . . ."

When sodium potassium passes through the reactor as the working fluid, it becomes highly radioactive. It carries the heat from the reactor to the boiler, creating steam for the turbines. That complicated process flashes through Lee's mind, as if he could determine in his country house the cause of the lethal leak in the ISC.

"Any radioactivity in the air-flow system?" Lee asks.

"Only traces, but you know how quickly seals deteriorate when they're not under pressure."

"So far we don't know if the seals have weakened."

"It's tricky to get at them. Some are buried inside the reactor wall."

"I know. They ought to be easily accessible for testing."

"Easily!" Rubikov explodes. "A little late for that statement. Those damn atomic engineers design everything as complicated as possible just to make sure nobody but themselves knows how to repair them."

"Is there any contamination outside the reactor globe?"

"I'm trying to measure that. I have a crew chasing around like rabbits with Geiger counters, running around everywhere—in the hotel, the labs, the hospital. Nothing so far, but that can change any second. Then what? Evacuate three thousand people?"

"Don't get upset, Ev. I'll be up as soon as I can, and we'll straighten out that problem together."

"It's your responsibility." Rubikov's voice is flat. "I just want to tell you."

"I bet you a case of vodka that everything will be fine."

"That's a lousy bet," Rubikov grunts, unappeased.

"If I win, we'll both be dead and you won't need to deliver!"

"If you can't lick this problem, nobody can." Lee produces a smile which has calmed many explosive situations. Rubikov's picture fades from the monitor.

Lee presses a number on the video dial. A girl's face appears.

"Dr. Powers!" she says, recognizing him.

"Get me Tomlinson," Lee says.

"The professor is at the hospital having a checkup. He didn't feel good this morning. Shall I connect you with his room?"

"No. Don't tell him I called." Lee shuts off the screen. Tomlinson should take a few weeks off, he contemplates. Lee knows that he too needs to rest. He has been on the ground only forty-eight hours, and his blood pressure is just getting back to normal; he'll need at least another forty-eight hours to feel all right.

Lee looks out of the window at the crystal blue water of the Lake of Thun, the chain of the Swiss Alps behind, the Jungfrau's eternally snowcapped peak, at the meadows looking almost artificial in sparkling green, unreal like the view of the mountain chain above them. He loves this small chalet, and he visits it as often as his duty allows. An old woman from the village cleans it. She is the only visitor permitted in this hermit's retreat.

The ISC is vulnerable. Though every part of it is 99.999 percent safe, Lee worries about the .001 percent which, multiplied by a hundred thousand different instruments and millions of parts, is a threatening factor. No mechanical device exists that is absolutely fail-safe. To evacuate three thousand people would take days. There are not enough astrocommuters and astrotugs built; there is not enough landing space for them on the ISC for a speedy evacuation.

"Typical of Tomlinson," Lee grumbles. "Waiting for me to leave the ISC to check in at the hospital. Hoping I won't find out. I'll make him take a long vacation, but on earth. He's getting on in years. Seventy! But will he ever retire?" Lee checks his thoughts, suspicious of his motives. He never trusts his conclusions when his emotions are involved. "Do I want him to stay around because I need him? What would I do without him?"

Gerald Tomlinson was once a professor of aeronautic research at Stanford University. He was Lee's teacher, Lee his assistant; then as Lee became prominent, the roles reversed. Tomlinson, though still engaged in space research, is in fact Lee's right-hand man.

Lee stuffs his pockets with tobacco and pipes, then leaves the chalet, closing the heavy door behind him. He looks nostalgically at the steep gabled roof slanting at a 60-degree angle, a protection against snow, which in winter covers the house up to the balcony.

On the meadow in front of the chalet, Lee's Hiller helicopter stretches its dragonfly rotors. It is a fast craft with a top speed of four hundred miles per hour.

Less than an hour later Lee sets the Hiller down on one of the landing rotundas of the Le Bourget spaceport.

The elevator in the Soleri cupola descends noiselessly. Its carpeted floor sinks three hundred feet below the ground. A diverse group of travelers fills the cubicle. The air is cool and pine-scented; soft Muzak is playing.

A young woman stands beside Lee. Her head reaches up to his shoulders and her hair has a luminous black Asian sheen. Lee can see part of her cheek, which is ivory pale as though she deliberately avoided the sun. She is dressed in a white suit of a glittering material that embraces her shoulders in custom-made perfection; a Paris dressmaker uses that fabric only for the superrich as a badge of exclusivity. Bothered by his nearness, she lifts her eyes; they are light gray like those of a bird of prey. For a second their gazes are locked together. She meets his eyes with an aloofness designed to ward off any male approach. Lee believes he has seen that striking face before but cannot place it.

His mind returns to Rubikov and the radioactivity problem. How can the ISC be made less vulnerable? Adding three more standby reactors to the existing three? Adding a second level in hangars, thus doubling the space for ferries to land? The answer always seems to be to add mechanical devices. But every new device carries its own failures.

The young woman abruptly turns her back to Lee, as if sensing the tension which Rubikov has transferred to him. Her body has a sensuousness Lee cannot define. Is it the proportion of limbs and torso or that intricate interplay between head, arms and legs, like the rhythm of a dance? Lee deliberately turns partially away from her. As if a man's inattentiveness were an insult to her, she suddenly steps closer. Again their eyes meet for a fleeting moment. His gaze, casual and absentminded, but still that of a male, conscious of a beautiful woman's presence, reassures her. He discovers a smile in her eyes, though her features do not change.

The elevator reaches the ground floor. As soon as the doors slide open, the black-haired woman hurries out past Lee. He remains in the elevator until the last passenger files out. A dozen men traveling from one continent to another via ISC with the ease of taking an autobus to another part of town; a dowager, hung with pearls, surrounded by a gaggle of extremely pretty girls, members of the Miss Space contest, the dowager obviously their chaperone. She carries a small dog that wears a collar made of precious stones. A harassed-looking young woman with a baby in her arms, and two small children trailing her, children born in an age that has lost conception of distance.

Lee walks slowly to the reception desk. There is no point in hurrying like the eager passengers. The space ferry, the astrocommuter, will leave for the International Space City in one hour and eight minutes on the split second to dock at the ISC twenty minutes after it crosses Paris.

Lee watches the young woman talk to the receptionist, a girl in the red uniform of the ISC. She passes a few notes, possibly messages, to the dark-haired one, who stuffs them unread into her handbag and walks on with a dancer's graceful movements. The passengers crowd the desk, checking in. Lee waits until the last one leaves, then steps up to the girl in the red uniform.

"A ticket for the next flight, please," he says unhurried.

"Your reservation, please." Without looking up, the girl stretches out a thin hand while punching keys on an intercom board with the other.

"I haven't got a reservation."

"The astrocommuter is fully booked for the next four flights. The best I can do for you is a seat on the six A.M. shuttle."

"I'm sure you'll be able to get me on this one."

Lee places an identification card in front of her. The girl looks at the card. Her head whips up.

"Dr. Powers! Why, I've seen your picture in every paper—"

"Every one?" Lee wishes the dark-haired woman had exhibited some of the clerk's enthusiasm.

The girl flushes. "I'll get you on the next shuttle. We'll just have to bounce one of the passengers; you have priority. That is, if it's urgent."

"I'm afraid it is," Lee says, his mind conjuring up the reactor, men in masks and protective clothing, moving silently like ghosts and sealing off a part of the ISC—a thought which constantly terrifies Rubikov.

"Let's see what we can do for you." The girl picks up the passenger list. "Number Eighteen seemed to be in a hurry to get to the bar. I don't think she'll mind waiting for a while."

Lee looks toward the end of the long corridor that leads to the departure gate. The ceiling is covered with a painting of the earth in Mercator's projection, with stylized cities, mountains and oceans. His eyes search for Switzerland, the town of Thun, its lake and his chalet, which the artist has whimsically added.

Lee fights a sudden impatience. His job is up there, at the ISC. The International Space City commanded all his energies and attention for years; only lately, after the huge satellite was completed, has he slowly become aware that he also needs a private life, in order to keep his mind in balance. He has bought the chalet in a part of the globe which is still rural, away from the thoroughfares of the world, and there he has found the only relaxation he has known in many years.

"You'd better get yourself a steady girlfriend," Tomlinson admonished him. "If I remember rightly, sex is a great antidote for tension. Play around a little, before you become a perambulating computer."

"Got any good telephone numbers?" Lee asked him, amused.

"You don't need them. You only have to be receptive when they call you. Believe me, sex and love are a world as large as outer space, maybe larger."

Tomlinson was married for forty years, until his wife died. Her death made him a hermit.

"A waste of time," Lee replied.

"Young whores, old nuns," Tomlinson said. "Or vice

versa. When that happens to you, I hope I'll be around to hear you complain of having wasted too much time on space research."

"So far I've found space sexier than any woman," Lee said and laughed.

Now, his body aching with a tension he cannot shake even in his sleep, Lee walks toward the end of the corridor. He forces his thoughts to wander, divorcing himself from his worries about the ISC.

Lee's thoughts return to the girl in white and her bird-of-prey eyes, aloof, detached, precious and conceited. A brittle challenge, which would divert him from the continuous demands of the ISC.

As he saunters toward the end of the long corridor, he passes the bar, a circular room with a high dome, glittering with laser beam decorations that cross and crisscross in geometrical pattern. Light becomes a substance, a conductor like a wire, a new dimension whose possibilities have only to be tapped. The bar is crowded with passengers waiting for the astrocommuter that will take them to the ISC.

"Miss Susanne Lesuer," a loudspeaker above his head whispers. There are dozens of them hidden in the ceilings of every room and corridor. "Miss Lesuer, please report to the reception desk."

He sees her again. She walks quickly toward him, and her eyes glance at him as she passes him hurriedly on her way to the reception.

Lesuer? Susanne? French? Lee has met Norwegian girls with dark Asian hair and light eyes. A mixture of Europe and Asia?

He watches her dancer's stride, the deliberation of her movements, as if nothing could stop her.

There is an argument which the receptionist parries with professional skill. Susanne Lesuer looks back in Lee's direction. Has the receptionist given him away?

Lee quickly walks on. He does not want to confront her and her anger.

At the door to the tube that shoots the shuttle into space, Lee flashes his identification for the guard.

"The ferry leaves in one hour, Dr. Powers."

"I know," Lee says impatiently. "Just let me in."

"There's that cargo ferry going first," the guard says, a bit awed by Lee's presence.

"I know. Just open up," Lee says curtly, passing the man. The door slides back. Lee enters the tunnel. He has the impression of standing inside a colored glass bottle sixty feet in diameter, whose neck disappears in the distance, out of his view. Electromagnetic plates are set into the ceiling and sides every two hundred yards; electrically charged, they propel the astrocommuter through the tube. When the shuttle breaks into the open, eight hundred and fifty feet above the ground and at a speed of five thousand miles per hour, it folds out its guiding fins and becomes a supersonic airplane. The fusion-based reactor system, eight hundred and thirty thousand pounds of hydrogen fuel, accelerates the craft to the speed necessary to reach the International Space City and to dock.

The building of the space city was completed right on schedule; even the financing was no problem, since the project was launched in a period of rapprochement of the major world powers. Every participating country was interested in contributing to the costly project; none wanted to be left out. The ISC is neutral ground, a visual symbol of unity of the countries on the globe, propagating peace. Lee has the disquieting feeling that the entire project went too smoothly; he does not want future difficulties to be covered up by a political euphoria. Can they be starting now when the ISC has been in space for only two years?

His steps echo along the tunnel which stretches for

five miles into the dark, slowly rising on a two degree slope, its exit high above ground. Lee feels empty, now that the work has become routine. Its challenges have narrowed down to problems which his staff can handle without him. The immense task of creating such a gigantic device that rotates the earth every ninety-five minutes leaves Lee burned out. Tomlinson, his alter ego, his father confessor and rock of Gibraltar in hours of despair and indecision, once formulated Lee's problem in an anecdote:

"You remind me of the man who bets he can eat fifty sausages. He eats forty-nine, decides he doesn't like them anymore, and orders an omelet. You've eaten your fiftieth sausage, Lee, and don't know where to go from here. Life is interesting only between expectation and fulfillment."

Lee hears a low, hissing sound at his side. An astrocommuter, its Vycor eyes muted, its pointed nose like that of a game fish, moves past him and stops. Its door slides back, painted white, it looks evil and efficient, streamlined like a man-eating shark.

Its cargo is mainly water, the most precious commodity on the satellite. The air of the ISC is constantly dehydrated, the liquid distilled for recycling. Even human liquid waste is put to use: heated under pressure, it is ejected into the outer space by small jets which control the ISC's rotation. A favorite joke among the designers is that the ISC keeps itself in balance by pissing into the void.

Can the ISC prove that the people of the world need no boundaries to work harmoniously together? That nationalism and chauvinism belong to a barbaric past? That idea was once behind Lee's obsession to create the City in the Sky. But so far his idealism remains unsatisfied.

Now that the giant satellite circles the earth every ninety-five minutes, Lee experiences the letdown of a dream that has not become reality. Ideologies have become sharply defined. The tensions between nations have not been assuaged. Computerized techniques do not bring peace to the world.

As Lee passes the astroferry, the tube suddenly flares up brilliantly. The white shark starts to glide slowly on small wheels, embedded in the tube; the activated electromagnetic plates pull the vehicle forward at increasing speed, rolling it away noiselessly. The first plates shut off, the current charging the second, then the third, the fourth and the rest in rapid succession, like lights on a string, flaring up and extinguishing. The shuttle gains speed, leaving a vacuum behind which surrounds Lee like a tiny tornado, almost turning him around his axis. Quickly, he retreats into one of the tube's recesses. The astrocommuter, blocking out the string of lights like a shadow racing past them, disappears with a roar. Valves in the ceiling and floor open to compensate for the vacuum, but he is still buffeted by the airstream swirling around him.

Lee's brain instantly clicks into action, devising a different solution to the sudden change of pressure. If compressed air would equalize the ferry's backwash, the vehicle's speed would also increase. Lee's mind passes through rapid calculation. The shock waves reverberating from the tube's end repeat the echo, thinning it out until it vanishes. They leave an oppressive silence in its wake, an emptiness as though the tube were located in space.

# III

"I'd like to take the ferry up myself; I'm still a dues-paying member of your union," Lee says to the pilot of the astrocommuter. "You must be exhausted from doing nothing. Take my seat, Number Eighteen. Be a passenger and relax."

The pilot, in his late thirties, bronzed, trim in his red space uniform, grins at Lee's unorthodox order.

"If you want to switch jobs, Dr. Powers, I'll gladly take yours, including the fringe benefits."

Lee gingerly lowers himself into the seat in the pilot's small compartment.

"You pilots are like parasites," he says, sighing. "Who needs you? The shuttle runs electronically. It's thoroughly programmed; it can't make mistakes. It's your union that forces us to keep you on. You're as obsolete as the firemen on diesel trains."

The pilot laughs, conforming to Lee's mood.

"Remember the tape we used to run before takeoff?" His voice becomes monotonous, rasping, as if coming through a bad loudspeaker. "This astrocommuter which is going to take you to the International Space City has been carefully programmed and computerized. It is absolutely fail-safe. Nothing can go wrong. There is no need to worry . . . no need to worry . . . no need to worry . . . no need to worry. . . ."

"That story was already tired when my mother nursed me," Lee says. "Okay, the tape gets stuck. That's why we don't use them anymore. Whatever we can eliminate can't go wrong. Pilots, of course, never make mistakes; they're the knights of space travel! Infallible, competent, reliable!"

Lee has been a test pilot for space shuttles. He has

flown hundreds of hours in different kinds of ferries and interplanetary space vehicles. Now, snugly confined in the small compartment, facing familiar batteries of instruments, he again enjoys the surge of power as his body integrates with the astrocommuter's great engines.

To balance the impersonal powers of the computers which govern the techniques of his profession, Lee practices mysticism. Now, inside the ferry's control room, he fuses with that force of one million, two hundred and fifty thousand pounds of thrust, becoming an integral part of the machine.

The seat, softly sculptured to his body, encompasses him. The safety belts are loosely draped around him; they will tighten automatically in case of sudden deceleration. A green row of lights on the dashboard indicates that the astrocommuter is ready for departure. The time is eleven six on the clock. Two minutes to go.

"See you at the ISC," the pilot says and salutes. The door to the compartment closes behind him. Lee is alone in soundless isolation. Again he experiences the excitement before taking off into space. He looks through the Vycor glass window toward the end of the tunnel ribboned like a Christmas tree with flashing red lights. The red changes to green.

Lee puts his hand on the manual emergency steering device. He feels a tiny shudder running through the stick as the ferry comes to life. Green lights shoot toward him, slowly at first, quickly changing into a blur and finally into a solid strand of light like a laser beam's. The plates, magnetized by electric current, accelerate the astrocommuter through the tube. The end of the tunnel appears, a pinprick of light, quickly changing into a glaring sun. Suddenly Paris lies under Lee's feet. The huge high rises of the twentieth century, Port Maine-Maillot's Convention Center towering over the Arc de Triomphe, the giant Montparnasse complex which ruptures the city's classic skyline, the Porte de Vanves, the monoliths of the Front de Seine, the fifty-thousand-seat sports stadium at the Parc des Princes, the Lariat of the Boulevard Périphérique encompassing the city, and like a telescopic lens zooming from close shot to infinite, Paris changes into a colored map, traversed by the glittering snake of the Seine River. Then Paris disappears as the stark glaring blue of outer space replaces it.

The astrocommuter streaks due east, gaining speed at the rate of fifteen hundred feet per second each minute, increasing its acceleration to rendezvous at the programmed second with the International Space City.

Lee's senses sharpen; his eyesight seems to become telescopic; a different awareness of his body makes him feel buoyant, quick thinking, as though the gravity of the earth were releasing his mind in space. Lee's ferry increases its speed and rises into the darkness of the void.

Lee checks the ferry's speed. It reads eighteen thousand miles per hour. His craft has flown twelve minutes since it left Le Bourget. A city appears, three hundred miles down range below him, covered by the misty smog of the earth: Stuttgart in Germany. Another four hundred miles and the astrocommuter passes Budapest. Odessa is to Lee's left, and in the distance, to his right, the toe of the Italian boot, flat and rugged like tissue paper torn unevenly at its edges.

A glittering speck of light climbs over the horizon at three hundred miles per minute. He traces the giant satellite on the instrument panel. It quickly gains in definition and size: the International Space City.

Lee becomes one with the ferry's computer. On his instrument panel he checks the bank of gauges, the pressure in the pilot's cabin, that in the storage and passenger compartments, the velocity of the ferry in relation to the earth and to the enormous glittering globes of the ISC, its silvery configurations connected by huge spokes. The ISC rotates at three revolutions per minute, a giant Ferris wheel. The hangar in its nose moves counterclockwise, staying vertical to the earth.

Lee measures his distance to the ISC. The ISC is two miles behind, approaching slowly, the letters *ISC* painted in giant lights on its sides. Lee listens to the celestial music emerge from the loudspeaker in his cabin, the ISC's theme song, endlessly repeated. It pinpoints its position for the tracking stations on the ground.

Seemingly close but still a hundred and eighty miles above Lee floats the Space Prison, the small replica of the ISC. The Space Prison was once a space laboratory, then Lee's headquarters during the construction of the City in the Sky. Lee proposed to dismantle it after it had served its purpose, but the major powers that had contributed to the construction of the ISC designated it as a space prison. To Lee it looks incongruously like a misshapen planet, inhabitated by nondescript people, expendables of earth's society, people too explosive to be kept on earth. But being human, they leave a mark in his conscience, which stays with him like a festering wound.

An orange flash on the shuttle control panels indicates that the astrocommuter is within the computer control of the ISC. Lee checks the yaw, the roll-and-pitch indicators on his control panel as automatically as a seasoned driver looking every few seconds in his rearview mirror.

He now is lined up with the ISC's orbit, his speed two miles slower than that of the space city. Pale bluish yellow spears of flame dart from Lee's astrocommuter's low-thrust engines. He depresses the command switch which programs the ISC's computer for the approach to the hangar. His craft will land in a few minutes. He watches through the Vycor window, capable of withstanding enormous heat generated when the shuttle reenters the earth atmosphere. Giant globes a hundred feet in diameter appear to roll toward him, enormous children's balls diving up from below. They lift themselves out of his vision to make room for another globular toy of the glittering giant.

The astrocommuter slows down to a crawl as the computer directs the ferry to Lee's right, toward the giant maw which is the hangar's door. The distance between the two spacecraft narrows; the giant hangar approaches Lee's ferry with the leisure of an old man's walk and swallows it.

The astrocommuter slides into the hangar's mooring; the gate of the ISC closes. Compressed air rushes in. The green light on Lee's instrument panel changes to amber. A tiny shudder runs through the craft. The astrocommuter has settled in the belly of the City in the Sky.

# IV

Pierre Bardou tilts his head and keeps his eyes half closed to protect them from the glare of the light stabbing through the plexiglass window of the Alouette helicopter. The expanse of houses below looks like flotsam bobbing in the murky tide.

The Arc de Triomphe floats by, broad avenues radiating from its base. The craft flies low, and Bardou can distinguish the flyspecks of people and the antlike crawl of buses and automobiles. They seem to move according to a mysterious system of chaotic order.

Bardou adds the picture of Paris's rooftops to the file in his mind, a mental photograph he wants to look at when *le cafard* becomes overpowering in the loneliness of the Space Prison.

Pictures imprint themselves in his memory, programming it like a computer. They emerge, seemingly haphazardly, shaping his consciousness by association—a smell and a human body, a touch and the face of someone long forgotten, a painting matching a landscape he once saw, a sound evoking a picture in his mind. The congruity of minute details triggers a recall to his senses.

Looking down at the sea of roofs, each one like a tiny village with towers and gardens, windows and pathways, soot-stained chimneys barren like trees after a forest fire, Bardou vividly remembers the face of a man condemned to death. Did he ever see him or only read about him? Where? In a newspaper? A novel? The death penalty was universally abolished years ago. The victim's features flash through his mind, palimpsest over a face Bardou cannot make out. Is it his own underneath the condemned man's features? The face he recalls is sallow like blotched parchment, chewing gum, the jaws working rapidly. With singular and brisk intent the convict walked up to the scaffold where the hangman waited, dressed in a tailcoat. Bardou does not recall the actual hanging, but the dull thud when the trap was sprung resounds in his ear.

The condemned man died before he went on his last walk. His mind stopped hours before the execution with a last image etched into his cortex. Perhaps a face of his past, a casual sentence or melody endlessly repeated, or some trivial impression, like smoking a cigarette, or the taste of his last meal, circled his consciousness like a needle on a record. The act of official killing was a physical act which had nothing to do with any awareness of the man whose neck was to be broken.

Bardou's mind too registered an image when the judge in Lyons sentenced him to spend the rest of his life in the Space Prison. The judge's face, bloated by wine and a food too rich for the liver and kidneys, stays with Bardou like a photograph.

In the seclusion of his cell the initial shock of his conviction faded away. A visionary thought replaced it, a daring idea which was going to shock and terrify the world, exonerate Bardou and give him back his freedom.

He has locked that ingenious brainstorm in the vault of his mind, to examine it in the seclusion of the Space Prison. To deceive his jailors, he plays the role of a man resigned to his fate.

"We're passing over the Ronde Point des Champs-Elysées," the guard at Bardou's side announces. His ascetic head, as if carelessly attached on an assembly line, does not fit the rest of his body. His voice is that of a man who studied elocution in evening classes.

"I'm a criminal lawyer by profession," the guard says as though answering Bardou's unasked question, "but I decided on this job ferrying people to the satellite."

He does not say "Space Prison." "I'm the guide for French citizens. Other nations, too, use our space ferries, but they send their own escort. I never get tired of that trip. When I leave the earth and its gravity, I don't feel shackled. My mind works much more clearly in space. We all are weighed down by troubles that drown our minds in mud. You too will enjoy that flight—that is if you can detach yourself from your thoughts and appreciate the moment. What is yesterday's news and what is tomorrow's? This reminds me of the priest who accompanies the man to the gallows and complains to him that he has to return home in that lousy weather while the condemned man doesn't." He chuckles at his own joke.

Bardou turns, surprised that the guard is trying to console him.

"You'll have leisure to write many books," the guard continues, with a quick, wan smile, "or whatever you want to do and never find enough time for it. No cells, of course, on that satellite. No use for them, Dr. Bardou. The food isn't anything to brag about. The main staple is alga, grown up there in hydroponic containers. It's short of vitamins, and I suggest that you order some from earth. Anything you want I will gladly bring up to you. Just remember my name! Jules Dubois." He waits politely for Bardou's reaction.

To please him Bardou mutters, "Thanks, Dubois. I certainly won't forget."

Dubois continues eagerly, trying to take Bardou's mind off dark thoughts: "From your vantage point at the satellite you'll be able to observe the stars above and the earth below, watch storms gather while you'll be serenely free of weather changes. There aren't any weather problems in space. The governments don't send any rabble up there; that'd be too costly. Those people around you are the revolutionary elite of the world. Society calls them misfits. Why? Just because they're ahead of their time and because their ideas and philosophies are endangering their society. Look who's running the world! A bunch of nitwits who wouldn't have a chance getting the job of running a medium-sized factory!"

"Careful." Bardou grins dutifully at him. "That's treason! They might send you up there, too!" His face, bleached by months of confinement, looks like parchment crumpled by a careless hand.

"No such luck!" Dubois exclaims. "I haven't got the brainpower to be honored that way." He bends forward until his face almost touches Bardou's. "You know, that's amazing. You've already got space eyes!"

"Space eyes? What's that?"

"People up there acquire that expression after a while, when they adjust to their situation."

"Adjust?" Bardou repeats. "Adjust sounds like permanence. Nothing is permanent as long as we're alive."

"A good thought," Dubois concurs and looks at Bardou with veiled envy as if he too would like to be sequestered in the Space Prison because of superior brainpower. "If nothing is permanent, then you won't be up there forever. Permanence starts with death. How's that for a philosophy?"

A dull pain in Bardou's side makes him sit up straight. An electronic device has been surgically implanted in his side below the left lower rib. His movements are monitored by the police on earth. He wears no handcuffs. Where could he run to? He would be traced within minutes.

So far only criminals have such a monitor attached to them. But international legislation is pending that would implant such a device in every person in the world. For safety reasons, should he get lost at sea or in the woods or lose his memory. Nobody has to fear his government if he stays within the law. Society has the duty to defend itself against its enemies and to safeguard its law-abiding citizens. That is the opinion of Bardou's judge in Lyons.

"The satellite isn't lonely." Dubois still watches Bardou's eyes in wonder. "There's even female companionship—that should add to the diversion. You'll find people up there the establishment considers dangerous: fascists from Russia and China, who also send up some of their poets. Communists from America and South America. The Russians used to throw their opposition into lunatic asylums; now they shoot them into space! You revolutionaries try to turn the world into a dull socialistic state. One man works; another man watches him, doing nothing, but he still gets paid. That's socialism! Full employment guaranteed! Income for everyone! Every one of those people up there has foolproof ideas on how the satellite should be run. What a mess! The prison is a microcosm of the confusion on earth! Since everybody believes that only he's found the panacea, no decision that satisfies all can be made." Dubois smirks, and his ascetic face looks vicious in its mirth. "You have to decide about a method of living, or ruling, or philosophy, but you must pick one, right or wrong. If you don't, you have chaos. I read some of your books. Just try to put your ideas into practice, Dr. Bardou, and you'll run into an opposition that will fight to the death!"

"Possibly," Bardou mutters, acting the part of the dejected prisoner. He watches the quickly approaching ground.

Le Bourget airport has been converted into a spaceport, which from the copter's height looks like a well-groomed park. The architects esthetically camouflaged the spaceport, hiding its purpose. Patches of greenery surround flower beds. Small landing circles for helicopters, cut out of the grass, are painted in pastel hues. A few of those colored areas contain helicopters, some in the process of taking off, others settling down like dragonflies. Minibuses, built like flat beetles, ferry passengers to the entrance, a Paolo Soleri cupola peering out of the ground. A huge silvery tube rises in a low angle eight hundred feet into the air, replacing the Eiffel Tower as the symbol of Paris. The tube guides the astrocommuters, the short-winged passenger spacecraft, into space. A landing strip ends at the oval mouth of a concealed tunnel, the entrance for the arriving astrocommuters and the astrotugs that carry freight. Except for the strange craft taking off and landing, the minibuses and small groups of people, nothing indicates that below the ground a spidery network of tunnels, rooms, offices and communications centers stretches for miles.

"A man with your mental capacity will never get bored wherever he is." Dubois talks like an ambulance driver taking a dying man to the hospital.

The copter descends on a mauve-colored rotunda. Its door swings open, and a narrow ladder unfolds from its belly. Dubois and Bardou climb out and walk toward the waiting minibus. Bardou looks at the sky with its gray ocean haze drifting in from Normandy. He fills his lungs as deeply as he can, expanding them with this air, moist, scented with the flavor of France, his country. The air in the Space Prison will be recycled, artificial, like the infinite space which is void of smell and sound.

"We have twenty minutes before our astrocommuter leaves," Dubois says. "You're the only passenger."

He says "passenger," not "prisoner."

# V

Stig Ibbotson plants his big bulk on a swivel chair behind his desk that protrudes leglessly from the wall. The convex soles of his canvas shoes suck lightly on the floor to keep him from floating. Behind him looms the eternal darkness of the galaxy, pinpointed by celestial bodies which might have exploded and died aeons ago, their light traveling on eternally.

The Space Prison whirls around the earth, which rises in Ibbotson's window every eight minutes, a giant sphere partly covered by clouds, snowcapped Alps, stretches of land appearing flat from the distance of five hundred miles above, as though the earth were as barren as the moon.

Originally built as a space laboratory, the prison contains its original amenities. The rooms are equipped with built-in functional furniture, sizable beds, indirect lighting, an ingenious heating and cooling system and every comfort the engineers could devise to make the astronauts' long stay in space bearable.

"Welcome to the space coffin," Ibbotson says to Pierre Bardou with gloomy pride. "Let me make one thing clear to you right from the start: I'm boss up here, chosen by democratic process. The word 'democracy' up here has many connotations. We all call it democracy, but some want it to be run by a democratic junta, some want a democratic dictatorship, some a democratic decentralization, ruled by democratic bosses. You'll never get those people to agree unanimously on anything. Of course we have secret elections. Secret! We know each other's views and know who casts what vote. I've been elected to head a committee of eight that runs the satellite."

Only half an hour ago the space ferry delivered Bardou to the Space Prison. Dubois turned him over to a black man in a karate gown. The man introduced himself in a cultured voice as Adar Kentu. He led Bardou down a corridor past closed doors.

"You were expected," Kentu said. "Your room is ready; I will show you where it is, in case the committee approves of you. If you continue walking from any point on the SP, you'll always return to where you started."

"Why does the committee have to approve?" Bardou asked, suppressing a sudden anxiety.

"Whenever Ground sends up a new inmate, one of the rooms has to be evacuated," Kentu said evasively. "We can't have more than sixty people up here." Kentu entered a small room whose door was open.

"We've watched your trial," Kentu said with sly appreciation. "You published secret government papers! Military treaties even the French Assembly didn't know about! How could you shock Europe that way? Welcome to the club of misfits!"

"Glad to find myself among members of my own ilk," Bardou said with a wan smile. "That makes me feel at home right away." He looked around the room. "This seems better than the cell in Lyon."

"Some of your belongings arrived with the space ferry," Kentu said with a vague gesture toward the empty bookshelves. "In a few days you'll have yourself established for the rest of your life." He hid a sudden restlessness, as if he wanted to avoid any familiarity with the newcomer.

"Stig Ibbotson is waiting for you. If you have questions, he will answer them."

Again passing closed doors, Kentu took Bardou to

Ibbotson's office. A few inmates in karate gowns watched Bardou inquisitively. One of them, a young woman, stared at him intently with a mysterious smile, like a man watching a woman he desires.

"Always remember that we didn't ask you up here," Ibbotson says to Bardou.

"Kentu told me that I'll have to be accepted by the committee. What did he mean by that?"

"You'll find out soon," Ibbotson says. His puffed face is hidden behind a beard of mottled gray, his large-lipped mouth is clean-shaven, and he bites his lips as if to punish himself for talking against his will. As he leans abruptly forward, his eyes adjust to Bardou's face like a camera lens bringing an object into sharp focus.

"We have no room for people who do not fit our setup. We can't keep them here, nor can we send them back to Ground."

"You mean you murder them?" Bardou gasps. There it is again, that warning of an imminent danger to his life which he sensed the moment he set foot on the satellite.

Ibbotson's eyes lose focus. "Murder? Up here words change their connotations. We have no alternative. Everyone up here has to have a function to keep life going. If he does not fit. . . ." Ibbotson shrugs with regret. "But I'm hopeful you'll be able to adjust yourself, a man of your intelligence." His faded eyes measure Bardou expertly. "Yes, a man of great intelligence; that's why you'll understand our predicament. Of course, we do that kind of thing very humanely."

"A humane death?" Bardou says. "Euthanasia! That word takes care of the guilt of people who stay behind."

"It does, if you feel any guilt." Ibbotson gives Bardou a hard, impatient look. "Dr. Behrmann uses a drug which produces euphoria. But I wouldn't worry about it, Bardou. If it happens to any of us, we won't know. So what's the difference?"

"Are you above the law?" Bardou explodes in an impotent rage. "I see! What could Ground possibly do to you? You're here for life, aren't you? There is no further punishment possible."

"We have sole jurisdiction up here; Ground doesn't interfere with us."

"Who passes judgment? Who decides who should live and who should die? Do you sign a death warrant? Make the murder a matter of record?"

"Nobody signs anything up here. The committee decides by majority vote. Ground just informs us that they are sending up another prisoner. If we get a prisoner without having room for him, we have to get rid of someone who has outlived his usefulness, or we can't accept the new arrival."

The radio on Ibbotson's desk emits a melody, faintly at first, increasing in strength, a pleasant pealing of notes, old-fashioned in a three-quarter time like that of a nineteenth-century dance. The sound gains in volume, filling the room with its repetitious tune.

Ibbotson suddenly comes to life, his ear eagerly bent toward the radio. "The International Space City. The ISC!" Spinning the swivel chair, he snatches a pair of binoculars from his desk drawer. "The ISC passes us twice a day, since we travel in almost the same orbit—but we are at a greater distance from the earth, so we move more slowly. Have a look at it! It's quite a sight!"

He tosses the glasses to Bardou, and they float toward him. Bardou catches them. One big step makes him glide to the window.

The ISC emerges from behind the curvature of the earth. It looks like a frail Tinker Toy, as it approaches, slowly filling the binoculars' field of vision, it looms gigantically. The construction, brilliantly reflecting the light of the sun, revolves around its axis three times every minute. Bardou loses sight of it, since the Space Prison also rotates. The ISC rises again in his glass like a metal whale diving from the ocean and submerging again. Disappears and rises.

Ibbotson's low voice is overcome by awe. "The ISC is the exact replica of this satellite, only a hundred times its size."

"Then you know where the atomic reactors are situated?" Bardou asks, keeping his glasses focused on the rotating leviathan.

"I can draw you every nook and cranny of every part of the ISC. We've been studying it for years. I could find my way around it blindfolded."

The geodesic globes are windowed, round giant spacescrapers; some reflect the light, others appear to be dark. Its docking hatch in front gapes like the mouth of a giant whale, spitting out an astrocommuter that floats toward earth in a graceful curve. The whale's maw stays open for an astrotug to enter. It then closes fanlike doors, like a camera's shutter.

Two space ferries hover at the docking hatch, waiting to be admitted with their cargo of passengers.

The glittering construction is a train of globes a hundred feet in diameter, connected by tubular spokes half their height. The spokes fuse with the axis, around which the giant space edifice rotates to create its own gravity.

Its tail glides into Bardou's view, a cluster of fan-shaped disks and antennas, tubes rotating counter-clockwise, in a fixed position to the earth below.

"Rendock," Ibbotson says with awe. "Rendezvous and docking. Rendock, a new word. Rendock, that's what they do, but the passengers can leave at any time."

The ISC passes. The melody from the radio fades

away like the tingle of bells on a sled passing in a dark winter night.

"That melody—it preys on my mind." Ibbotson holds out his hands like a beggar. "It follows me in my dreams. It's torment to be cooped up here!"

Brutally including Bardou in his misery, he adds: "You will never be able to get out of here, Bardou. They won't permit anybody from up here to tell the world what it means to be a prisoner in space."

Bardou stretches painfully. His side hurts, and he puts his hand on it.

"You too are tortured by that infernal gadget," Ibbotson remarks with curious satisfaction. "Ground keeps a constant check on us, as if we could run away from here. We're dogs on a leash. Damn them, damn them!"

"Are these rooms bugged?" Bardou probes the plastic walls, the tied-down furniture, with his eyes. The pen on Ibbotson's desk, screwed into its holder to prevent it from floating away, might hold a listening device.

"We probed every inch of the satellite." Ibbotson walks to his chair, the soles of his shoes emitting sucking noises. Supporting himself on stiff arms, he bends conspiratorially toward Bardou. "We have a whiz in electronic devices, José Miranda. José once threw a bomb at the President of Portugal. I'm glad he did; we need him. José even built special detecting devices; he's very good at that, too. But he couldn't find anything. *Nada!* Ground isn't interested in our conversations; for them our files are closed. They're afraid if they listened to us, they might hear evidence that might revive some cases. They wouldn't want that. Every country is afraid of world opinion. We have a few innocents up here, people who shouldn't be here at all. Like Shepilov, the Russian poet. Sentenced to imprisonment for writing sonnets that displeased the socialist government, the government of the people! Does that make sense?"

As though talking to himself, he does not expect an answer. Ibbotson! That name suddenly enters Bardou's memory. He tries to visualize Ibbotson's face without a beard.

"Didn't you give that socialistic government information about the Western defense installations when you worked for NATO?"

An amused flicker appears in Ibbotson's eyes.

"Thanks for remembering me! I do have a kind of notoriety, which is the same as having fame, isn't it? The British government called me the worst spy who ever hit the Western defenses. What I did was burst open its flank. What I told the Russians helped establish the military balance between the superpowers. The military become very callous when they believe they have the upper hand over any adversary. They drag us into wars—that's how the generals get their promotions and higher pensions. Without wars they make less money when they retire. You can only stop them when they are afraid for their own hide. Do you think my crime warrants life imprisonment in space? I should be up for the Nobel Peace Prize instead!"

Bardou hears a sucking noise of steps approaching and quickly turns. The chair he is sitting on almost turns in a circle. A group of people walk in, among them the tall young girl who looked at him with unconcealed interest. She is olive-skinned, extremely well built, wearing a very brief skirt, exposing long, slender legs. She has changed her outfit as if to impress him sexually. Her dark eyes shine with cynical amusement from under a round forehead. The other woman is middle-aged, her face as wrinkled as a parched riverbed. The men are dressed in loosely fitting togas and flared trousers like karate fighters. They are of all ages and have the pallor of shut-ins. Among them are Van Buren, Hallstadt and Kentu.

Half-floating, which gives their movement a graceful air, they glide into Ibbotson's office.

"Meet the committee." Ibbotson swings his chair toward the wall to make room.

"My name is Miranda," a brown-skinned, muscular man says, and settles down on the floor, his legs crossed. "I'm in charge of the atomic reactors. I need an assistant. Do you have any experience in nuclear physics?"

"I'm a professor of semantics and taught social science; I also worked as a political adviser for the French government," Bardou says dryly.

"Social science? That's a science nobody can define," another man says, making it clear that he does not approve of Bardou's profession. "I'm Shepilov. My profession is being a poet. Now I'm up here writing space poetry and being trained to become a surgeon by our chief cutter." He vaguely nods toward an older man at his side.

"Behrmann, MD." That man introduces himself with a grunt. "Do you have any knowledge we can use up here? One has to be a specialist in something so we can run this place; otherwise he's useless to us. And we can't feed any idle mouths."

"That's what Ibbotson told me." Bardou feels himself surrounded by hostility. These people might have warped conceptions of values, having become compulsives in their shut-in loneliness. A man imprisoned on earth can hope to be paroled. He might become a "prison lawyer," studying law to find a loophole which will permit him to fight for his freedom. But the people around Bardou wait solely for their span of life to run out.

"I'm afraid I have no technical knowledge," he continues calmly, hiding his fear. "But I could be trained, I guess!"

The faces around him are stamped with an unearthly fourth-dimensional quality, the strange look Dubois remarked about when he spoke of "space eyes."

Bardou's gaze meets that of the tall, olive-skinned girl, who returns an intimate, seductive smile. She is the only one who seems to have kept a sense of earth normality.

"All right, we'll try to train you," Adar Kentu says. "That is, if you can be trained."

"Even a chimpanzee can be trained, but I might bring you an idea better than making a mechanic of me," Bardou answers.

He has the impression of being surrounded by a strange tribe of aborigines.

He gets up, stretching his slim, lanky frame; the loss of earthly weight gives him a pleasant feeling of elation despite the tense situation.

"That's a new approach," Behrmann says. "A good idea might be more useful to us than a man who can run a computer. What is it?"

"I also have my conditions," Bardou says. He has to convince these people, or he will lose out.

"Conditions?" Ibbotson seems startled by Bardou's forceful demand. "What conditions?"

"If you accept my idea, I want to organize it. That would mean you have to take orders from me. There won't be any room for discussions. I had a few months to think about it; I don't want any interference."

"That means we make you the boss?" Ibbotson asks dryly and laughs. "Most people lose their minds up here. Now they send us one who's already lost his on earth."

"You don't know his idea yet," the tall girl says. "Let's decide after we hear it."

A fat man with a pronounced Latin face enters the discussion. "You must have a powerful reason to make that suggestion. What could you offer that we can't?"

Bardou turns to the man, whom he recognizes as a former South American President. Carefully he says, "You're Alemán Guzmán; they threw you out of Ecuador. Didn't you run that country for a while?"

"We're discussing you, not me," Guzmán says impatiently. "I'm familiar with your political essays. You were a dangerous man, but you won't be dangerous to us. We'll see to that."

There is a threat in his rasping voice. "Politics won't get you anywhere up here at the SP. We don't need a professor of abstract social sciences to tell us what to do."

"My idea is to get all of us out of here," Bardou says flatly. "I'm sure you think you've considered every possibility, but mine is different—it's going to work."

He scans the hostile faces for a reaction.

Hallstadt replies, a malevolent grin hovering around his mouth, "I fought in Africa for freedom. They called me a mercenary since I got paid for risking my life. I've died a thousand times, and once more wouldn't make any difference to me. Of course, we've all had ideas how to leave the SP. How do you want us to die, Bardou?"

"I don't want you to die," Bardou says, speaking calmly now that he has made contact with at least one man. "I've been working on this plan since I suspected I might be sent up here."

"You'd better be explicit," Kentu says. "We've run into all kinds of schemes. Some even tried to make private deals with Ground, spying on some of the inmates." He speaks with the cultured accent of an Oxford education. "They didn't last. You can't keep a secret up here for long."

"So what's your carefully worked out plan?" Hallstadt asks, dangerously calm. He settles on the floor, holding onto one of the table legs to counteract his buoyancy.

"Kentu just told me that some of you can't be trusted. Do you want me to give away my idea without knowing if you're reliable? What guarantee do I have that after exposing my idea I won't be dragged to the air lock and thrown out?"

The tall girl says in a low, throaty voice, "I suggest that we take a vote first. I'm for accepting him. He can be fitted into our community even if his suggestion doesn't work out."

"I'm for letting him stay." Guzmán seconds her. "His political dissertations made sense to me, though our ideas oppose each other. I can't help believing that I'm here partly on account of his writings."

"I am going to make my decision after he has told us," Ibbotson says.

"I'm for him," Hallstadt says. "So is Van Buren, aren't you, Jan?"

The tie between the two men is obvious. Van Buren turns his angelic head to Hallstadt, smiles and nods.

"That's four votes. Why don't we make it unanimous?" the young woman asks.

"All right." The older woman at Guzmán's side speaks up for the first time. "I am for him. That makes five. Now you're safe, Dr. Bardou. You can speak up."

Bardou tries to get up but sinks back in his chair, attacked by a sudden, curious fatigue he has never experienced before. He moves the swivel chair close to the wall. Catching the large, liquid eyes of the olive-skinned girl, he speaks directly to her.

"I won't give out my information right now. But let me repeat that I know how to get out of here and be accepted by Ground, to live on earth. And not behind bars. But I can't face all of you at this moment. I'm too tired. If I'm supposed to be here a lifetime, give me the courtesy of getting some rest."

The words pour out of him under the pressure of his curious exhaustion. His eyes glide over the faces of the people, and he finds human response only in the face of the olive-skinned girl.

"I suggest we extend his lifetime until tomorrow," Kentu says. "But then he will have to talk and make some sense."

"He just got accepted by the majority." The girl puts her hand on Bardou's arm. He discovers a gleam of humor in her dark eyes as she supports Bardou to get up.

"You need somebody to take you to your room." She smiles, exposing impeccable teeth. "These people here are scared. Fear makes them act cruelly." The mocking expression does not leave her face. "My name is Cypriana. Cypriana Maglaya."

# VI

Bardou, floating in his space capsule, is racked by a fury that guides his thoughts, streaks of logic intermingling with fantasy. Half-conscious, he ponders which of the people he met in Ibbotson's office he can trust.

In his half dream names pass through his sleep-fogged memory: Ibbotson, pompous, jealous of his position as the leader of the inmates. Behrmann, the physician. Why has he been sent to the Space Prison? Shepilov, the poet. Is he a poet? Is he Russian as he claims? The expert on atomic reactors, Miranda. Is it true that he threw a bomb at a President? A bomb thrower and an atomic engineer? Not a very likely combination.

Bardou, between sleep and consciousness, examines the thoughts which pass through his mind. An on-looker. An onlistener. Being present and absent at the same time. That tall girl with the flowery name. Cordelia? Cypriana? Cypriana! What could her crime have been? All inmates are confined to the Space Prison for life. Bardou's inner fury increases, and he forces himself to wake up.

He remembers collapsing on the bed in the room assigned to him, as though under the influence of a powerful drug. The last image he remembers is that of Cypriana's large black eyes staring at him.

He has shed his coat, shirt and shoes but does not remember when. A blanket covers him. As he turns his eyes to the ceiling, a bland, smooth, plastic surface, the sudden night of the rotating satellite descends. Artificial illumination at once replaces the darkness. Slowly he turns his head and discovers Cypriana sitting on the floor, deeply immersed in reading a book.

She is naked. Her bare olive-skinned body fits the unreality of his half sleep. Her skin is without blemish. Her shoulders are childlike thin and square. Around her are unopened packing cases which Ground sent up before his arrival. She holds the book in curiously long, spidery fingers, the silvery polished nails groomed like those of a medieval Chinese noblewoman.

She is reading Bardou's book *The Broken Branch*, essays on man's flirtation with his own racial genocide.

With detached curiosity Bardou studies the girl, her heart-shaped face, too elongated to be truly beautiful, the fine bone structure tautly covered with a skin of near transparency, the mouth too thin to be sensual. Long black hair, carefully groomed, falls over both shoulders like a densely woven cloak. Her neck is extremely long, her breasts small and firm like those of an adolescent girl. Her waist is slender, her thighs rounded, slightly heavy, pubic hair blending with olive darkness. The shins of her long straight legs are shiny, hairless.

Her eyes are lowered, the lashes dense curtains. An artificial light shines behind her head, becoming electronically brighter as the shadow of the earth creates its short artificial night.

Bardou resents her presence. Why should she be naked, here in his room?

He sits up. At once her eyes lift, and unconcerned about her bareness, she puts down the book. "I wish you'd slept another half hour and let me finish." She shakes her hair with a willful, childlike motion. "No wonder they sent you up here. What a disdain for the human race! Reading your book, a person wants to commit suicide."

"It's one of my early books," Bardou says, moving to the edge of his bed, disturbed by the reduced weight to which he is not accustomed. Inertia makes him float for a second.

Cypriana's smile seems like an expression which might have shaped her features when she was in her teens. "You fell asleep as if you'd been hit with a hammer." She gets up, carelessly pushing away a heap of her clothes. "It happens to newcomers. A sudden imbalance of oxygen makes them black out. You'll get used to it and learn to cope with it."

As she stands up, Bardou becomes aware how beautifully she is proportioned, supported by an equilibrium of limbs and bones which sculptors rarely achieve.

She sits beside him on the bed, her long fingers close to his face without touching it.

"Forget your puritanism," she says, sensitive to his resentful reaction. "You're not in mortal danger from me! I just don't like to cover my skin, and mostly I move around naked. That is, if I don't have to work in the hospital. There are virtually no germs up here, but if you needed your appendix out, I'd be scrubbed, sterilized and wearing a white uniform. Dr. Behrmann let me operate once. The patient is still alive. But you might feel safer when I'm dressed." She fishes for her clothes with toes as movable as fingers. "You mention in your book that the human race is basically paranoid, that man as a species has the wish to disappear. And that he has a constant longing to die. You even claim that he hates every moment he's alive."

"Doesn't he, basically? Just give him time! He will succeed," Bardou says sarcastically to cover the incongruity of discussing his book with a naked girl. "He certainly is trying, though he makes it deliberately tough for himself to wipe out his species. Sexual abstinence and cyanide would do a faster job."

She takes his hand and studies it like a fortune-teller,

then puts it on her thigh without any sexual implication, as if wanting to gain his confidence.

"Was that really why you were sent up here? Because you published top-secret papers?"

"You know that wouldn't be cause enough for a life sentence, but the police conveniently discovered a cache of weapons buried in my house. They planted them there, of course."

"There was a shooting at the courthouse in Lyons," Cypriana announces like a prosecuting attorney. "Two of the jurors were shot."

"I was inside the building at the time. But my wife was outside picketing the courthouse with a group of my friends. She was killed by a stray bullet. Do you believe in stray bullets?"

"Accidents are very common if they are prearranged," Cypriana says. "We all know the right answers, but we're reluctant to face them." She covers her breasts with her arms in sudden shyness, then picks up a thin pair of pantyhose. "I hoped you'd sleep with me, but it doesn't seem to be working out."

"Making love in half gravity must be quite an experience." Bardou cannot suppress his cynicism, his only defense against the girl beside him, whose motives baffle him. "I didn't know there was a position I haven't tried. I had to be sent into space to get such an opportunity." He stretches out his hand, but she moves out of his reach. Solemnly she starts to dress. Her angular movements betray an insecurity she might not have had when she entered his room.

"Sleeping with you has nothing to do with making love to you. I'm not even physically attracted to you. You don't like me either."

Looking at her long, tapered back, Bardou quickly puts on his shirt. "That I'm not your type I understand. But don't be so sure about my not liking you."

"I don't want to offend you," Cypriana says without a trace of excuse in her low voice, "but the only way I can get free of this death house is to become pregnant. World opinion wouldn't permit a child to be born up here, and I have enough friends in high places to raise a fuss at the United Nations if I do conceive. Ground would have to ship me out of here."

"Why pick me to be the father?" Bardou distrusts her motives. "You have the choice of sixty men, most of them better-looking and probably better lovers than I. They might have better brains. Don't you believe in genetics?"

He tries to sound jocular and to dispel the picture of her nakedness which lingers in his mind.

"I've tried them all." Cypriana almost breaks under the strain of despair. "At first I thought it was my fault. But Behrmann made tests—I'm as sound as a mother cow and a natural to become pregnant. But all the men up here are sterile."

"*All* of them?" Bardou asks, startled. "Did Ground sterilize them before they shipped them up?"

"Behrmann says there's some kind of cosmic radiation that kills the sperm."

"And you wanted to use me before those rays can take effect on me? Your idea has a kind of logic."

"Yes. But you have a virginal streak." Her thin, passionate face with the oversized eyes betrays a glint of humor. "I have to be a fast worker." She steps close to him and puts her arms around him. "Besides, you interest me as a man. You're intelligent, and you're flexible in your mind. I hate people with rigid beliefs. You're creative—you said you came to us with an escape plan that might work. Can you tell me?" Her dark eyes squint as she looks at him.

Bardou still cannot suppress his suspicions about her behavior. "My idea is a kind of fancy suicide. We might die together. You wouldn't like that, would you?"

She shrugs and takes both of his hands in hers. "I don't think it would matter to you any more than it would to me."

Her unhappiness is like a darkness in the air.

"Assuming you become pregnant. Ground might force you to abort, then send you back!"

She looks at him wisely. "Of course I thought of that possibility. But would they dare to abort me forcibly? They could, of course, and pretend I miscarried. But the world would be in sympathy with me. The junta wouldn't dare ship me up a second time."

"How can they send a young girl like you to such a place?"

"I killed my father." Cypriana's even tone reminds him that she has been trained as a nurse. She is used to dealing with life and death on equal terms. "Premeditated. Cold-blooded. And justified." She sits down on the bed and lifts her large eyes at Bardou. They show no emotion. "My father ran for the Presidency of the Philippine Republic. He was liberal. Beloved by everybody. He won by a landslide. The hope of the people was on him. I thought he was a saint."

"But you killed him."

"I even helped him write his inauguration speech—that was how close we were. He had very little contact with anybody else, not even my mother. Soon after he became President, I found out he'd been groomed for that job by a secret group of powerful people. Only money is truly international. Money does not fight among itself."

She talks as if delivering a lecture she has repeated many times. "My father's image had been carefully prepared. His attitude, even toward me, was artificially created. As soon as he was elected, he hid in the Presidential Palace. Nobody but his bodyguards could get to him. Except me. I confronted him when he disbanded the liberal youth group of which I was a leader. His arguments were that people aren't important—only wealth is. He said the country's wealth would be concentrated in a few hands for a time, but it would finally seep down to lower levels and everybody would be comfortable. He forced me to leave the country, to study in England. On a holiday visiting him, I smuggled a gun into the palace and shot him dead."

Her round forehead glistens with moisture as she turns her tortured face to Bardou. "When we're young, our emotions tell us: yes, yes, no, no! After he was dead, I saw what I had accomplished. Nothing! A military junta took over. They wanted to put me in a lunatic asylum. But they feel safer locking me up here. For life!"

"Governments don't always last forever. You might be paroled, Cypriana." For the first time he calls her by her name. "I have a daughter your age. I am going to see her again. Don't ever think I'd let them stop me!"

Getting up, he balances waveringly. "Could you tell me who is reliable among the sixty men up here?"

"None is," Cypriana says. "All of them are ruled by fear. Fear of becoming useless and being eliminated by the committee. If you're smart, Dr. Bardou, take advantage of their insecurities. You're still in possession of your willpower. That might change when you've been up here for a time. Force your will on them! Don't let anybody dominate you. And never trust any of them."

"What about you?" Bardou asks. "Should I trust you?"

Cypriana smiles at him, the smile of a conspirator. "What would the alternative be?" The row of perfect teeth complements her smile. "You depend on me, and I depend on you. Take a chance on me!"

Bardou is aware that he is traveling the road of no return. "You might end up shooting me as you did your father."

"I might," Cypriana agrees. "If you deceive me, I'll want to shoot you. But nobody up here has a gun."

# VII

The prison's inmates crowd the spoke that leads to the commissary. That room also serves as a meeting place for the committee.

The spoke situated in the half-gravity segment has handles and straps protruding from its walls to keep people from floating helplessly. The outside walls are semitransparent, cutting the sharp light of empty space to a milky dusk, darkening completely when the satellite is covered by the shadow of the earth.

Bardou counts about fifty faces turned toward him and Cypriana, who walks at his side. He is running a gauntlet of mute hostility. Are those tormented faces, the pale features, the tense bodies, the same containers which once harbored progressive minds: scientists, social thinkers, political theorists, innovators of a world to come? Every new arrival is an intruder not to be trusted.

The door to the commissary is open. Ibbotson, his impressive bulk draped around a chair, is lecturing. He ignores Bardou when he enters; he is playing for position, sensing Bardou's superiority of mind.

"I contacted Ground by videophone," Ibbotson's voice whispers from hidden speakers. "Ground is reluctant to increase our ration of fresh vegetables. I told them that the diet of algae lacks the necessary vitamins. They want to cut down on essentials. We are dependent on Ground and can only plead. We have no power to put on any pressure. Or have we?"

There is no reply from the crowd. A deadly inertia, a lethargy that sees no hope for the future has burned out their initiative.

Bardou walks toward Ibbotson, past people strapped to the walls by safety belts. As he passes

Miranda, he is aware of an almost tangible air of hatred, perhaps because of Cypriana's interest in him.

Only now Ibbotson pretends to discover Bardou.

"Pierre Bardou, our new addition! I didn't expect him to join our weekly meeting. I thought he was busy in bed with Cypriana."

His coarseness annoys Bardou, and he glances at the girl, who holds her head rigid with contempt.

"As it happens, I was not in bed with Dr. Bardou, though that's none of your damned business, Stig, or anybody else's," she says. "Dr. Bardou told you that he has a valuable suggestion to discuss or he wouldn't join this futile session. Nothing ever will come of anything as long as Stig is conducting our business with Ground."

"Let's go to my office," Ibbotson suggests, trying to hold onto a position which is slipping out of his grip.

"We're going to stay right here, in the commissary," Bardou says flatly. "How do I know your office isn't bugged so that you can send a tape to Ground?"

Ibbotson bridles and lowers his bull's head as if wanting to attack Bardou bodily.

The older woman, Vera Stern, seasoned by a tolerance which age has given her, intercedes.

"If your suggestion is as strong as your suspicion about our committee, I expect to hear a very sound idea from you, Dr. Bardou. I've heard many, and none of them was workable. Ground isn't receptive to dealing with us. We even threatened mass suicide. That seemed to please them more than scaring them."

Vera Stern, an Englishwoman in her middle fifties, hefty and large-boned, was once a physicist working on secret electronic devices. She passed information to Israel, withholding it from her own government. Though the discoveries—amplifying ultra-minute electronic impulses into audible decibles—were her own, the British government banned her to the Space

Prison for life. The irony of her case is that the devices implanted in the space prisoners are based on her research.

But she maintains a singular and unusual relation with Ground. Ground supplies her with every electronic device she needs for her experiments. Self-contained and taciturn, she is continuing her research as if the change of venue from earth to space were only a slight inconvenience.

Ibbotson adjourns the meeting.

The prisoners begin to drift reluctantly away as if the disposing of time were the only objective of their existence.

Bardou looks around the commissary. It contains the former space laboratory's kitchen, the shortwave ovens, the ice makers, plate sterilizers and dishwashers like those of a luxury hotel. The plastic tables are fastened to the floor. The room, like the whole satellite, is pleasantly air-conditioned. One could live comfortably on a place like this, Bardou muses, if there were stairs leading back to earth.

The nine committee members gather around the table. The men look at Bardou guardedly, a platoon of conspirators mistrusting a possible spy.

"Now since you demanded a secret session," Ibbotson says, "I assume you'll have to trust us with your important secret."

Bardou has reached the point of no return.

"If my idea leaks out, we'll be a lot worse off than we are now. We might regain our freedom, or all of us might die."

"Very dramatic!" Shepilov enjoys the situation like a reporter confronted with an exciting scoop. "I'd take that chance!"

"I know how to get you out of here," Bardou says, watching the faces around him tighten in disbelief.

"That's nothing new; everybody up here has had

schemes," Hallstadt says. "I bet you want to skyjack one of the ferries that bring provisions and water."

"Exactly!" Bardou scans hostile and disappointed faces.

"Where would you fly it to? To Mars?" Ibbotson asks, bored. "If we go back to earth, we commit suicide."

"Certainly not to Mars, the moon or earth," Bardou says mysteriously.

"Have you discovered a new planet where we could land?" Adar Kentu sneers, leaning back in his chair like a member of a lynch jury. Bardou searches for Cypriana's eyes; she is the only one in whom he finds an eagerness to understand.

"You've heard of hijacking and of skyjacking. I'd like to add another word to the vocabulary: spacejacking!"

"Spacejacking!" Ibbotson exclaims with a look of appalled interest. "Spacejacking what?"

Bardou smiles slowly. He hums the melody the International Space City emits, the pleasant tune, old-fashioned like a nineteenth-century waltz.

Startled, the members of the committee seem frozen in their seats.

"You suggest spacejacking, as you call it, the ISC?" Mrs. Stern says.

"Spacejacking the International Space City! I admire your boldness, Dr. Bardou."

"The ISC isn't prepared for such an invasion," Bardou says quietly. "I understand it isn't armed at all, by international agreement."

"Nor are we," Kentu says, his furious fingers tearing up a piece of paper he is playing with. "Also by international agreement."

"We'll have to construct weapons." Bardou turns to him. "We have plenty of time."

"Your plan is arbitrary," Miranda says. "You haven't got the answers."

"Of course I lack technical know-how, but we have experts on the SP who could work out every step of my idea. Let's approach this problem like a chess game. If we make the right moves, we'll get out of here."

"If we occupy the ISC," Cypriana interjects with an overtone of admiration for Bardou, "we could threaten to shut off the atomic reactors. The ISC would freeze up within a day or two."

"And three thousand people with it." Shepilov crosses over to her conception.

"We too would end up as a block of ice," Ibbotson says stubbornly. "Who wants to die?"

"You're already dead, Stig!" Cypriana snaps. "You just haven't noticed. If we succeed, you'll rise out of your grave like Lazarus."

"I've been here for almost two years, and this is the first suggestion that's made any sense," Hallstadt says. "You can count on me, Bardou."

"Let's assume we succeed in occupying the ISC," Mrs. Stern says speculatively. "What will we do next? Try to make a deal with Ground? They'll agree to anything we demand. Why shouldn't they? As soon as we land on earth, we'll be arrested."

"Why should they stick to a deal?" Ibbotson gives Bardou a look of veiled triumph. "Your idea sounds good, but it won't work."

Cypriana's hair falls forward from her nape and hides her face. When she pushes it back, she looks grim with determination.

"They wouldn't dare double-cross us. The ISC is vulnerable. It's a three-hundred-billion-dollar international investment. We'll let Ground believe we have friends who will wreck the ISC if Ground breaks its agreement. They won't know if that's true or not, and they wouldn't dare risk it."

"We carry those electronic devices," Behrmann soberly reminds the group. "The moment we leave the SP, Ground will know and warn the ISC. Then we couldn't land on it."

"We'll find a solution to your objection, Doctor," Bardou says irritably. "Damn it, a thousand questions have to be solved. Did you expect me to arrive with a foolproof battle plan?"

"About arms," Hallstadt says cautiously, and with sly deliberation, "those can be easily manufactured."

"We'll need TNT, dynamite, plastic explosives," Ibbotson objects. "You can't make them up here. Ground is careful what kind of material they send us. Are you going to ask for trinitrotoluene?"

"We'll use compressed air," Hallstadt says. His sunburned brown-spotted face looks mysterious and diabolic in the white light that penetrates the room.

"Compressed air? You want to use air guns?" Ibbotson laughs. "Don't be ridiculous! Those are children's toys!"

"Are they?" Hallstadt grins at him. "I've made for myself a close-range weapon which works up to fifty feet with deadly accuracy. It penetrates a wooden plank one inch thick. A plastic bullet is inserted in a quarter-inch tube that contains high-pressure gases. Each weapon contains seven of those missiles. They start comparatively slow since they're rockets, but they gain maximum speed rapidly. The gun is only six inches long and one inch in diameter. I've made only one so far, but we could produce a hundred!"

The committee listens to him in shocked silence. "Why did you make that gun?" Ibbotson finally asks. Hallstadt's revelation touches a closed spot in his mind. "To kill all of us?"

"I feel vulnerable without a weapon," Hallstadt says

dryly, "really naked with all you murderers around me. One of these days when I've outlived my usefulness to the SP, you'll drag me to the air lock. Then you'll get your surprise! Two or three ounces of pressure on a gun trigger changes things drastically." His eyes are cold with fury. "I've never trusted you, Stig, or anybody else on the SP. You may thank me for that now. My suspicion about all of you has a practical effect—I know how to make a deadly gun with the material available to us. For me, killing contains the ultimate excitement. It's my religion!"

"We should send for a minister for you. Ground could supply one—one with a history of revolution. They are around, Hallstadt!" Shepilov says, his gaze lowered at the mercenary's jaw. "How much blood and death there are in the minds of people who claim to be religious! To kill for the good of mankind! How righteous! How saintly!"

"I am mankind," Hallstadt answers heatedly. "So are you, Shepilov. Your pacifism brought you here. Are you going to join us, or are you staying behind to put our experiences on the SP into blank verse?"

"I'll come along and write a poem about the struggle for our freedom."

"I propose that Dr. Bardou replace Stig as the head of the committee," Cypriana says.

Ibbotson's eyes open wide with fury.

"I suspected that bitch would turn against me as soon as she found a new stud to please her. I'm elected for four years. I'll be damned if I'll voluntarily resign. Besides, I don't believe Bardou's plan will work. We'll all die on account of it."

"Before we put Bardou's suggestion to a vote," Guzmán injects calmly, "we'll examine it carefully. In the meantime I propose to give Bardou all the powers he wants to realize his plan. Nobody ever came up with a concept like his. If he wants to run the show, let him!"

"He will be responsible," Van Buren says.

"And you won't be around if the spacejacking turns sour, Jan," Ibbotson says with sarcasm. "You'll have a hard time getting back at him. Because you'll be dead!"

"I second Guzmán's suggestion," Hallstadt says with a glance at Van Buren, who nods at him.

"Agreed," Shépilov says.

"No objection from my side," Miranda adds.

"Agreed!" Kentu seems to explode with impatience. "We don't need Stig's consent. The committee decides, not he."

"If you want to commit suicide, go ahead," Ibbotson says, shrugging exaggeratedly. "There's no use warning you. How can you warn dead people?"

# VIII

Middle section, Globe 5, gravity 0.2, adjoining the landing hangar is a restricted area, except for personnel dressed in blue, trousers striped white, holding security pass blue, to be carried on left side of the chest.

Kenneth Andrews—Kenny to Lee Powers and the security forces—sits like a spider on a swivel chair in front of the control consoles. On his right side Gay Chan, on his left Mahadma Indru watch the thirty TV monitor screens.

The screens can be switched to project almost a thousand different locations in the ISC. The hotel lobby, the hospital, machine rooms, storerooms, atomic reactors, the corridors, the hangar and various other places are under constant surveillance, watched by rotatable TV cameras. The cameras are tamper-proof. Anything touching them without authorization sets off an alarm in the control room. Almost two thousand locations aboard the ISC converge on the master console which is being monitored by a crew of three. Except for the private hotel rooms and the crew's sleeping quarters, all activities of the City in the Sky are uninterruptedly transmitted and taped in Room 500.

Antonio Ferranti, electronic engineer, the fourth man, is enclosed in his seat as if poured into it, in front of a second table that contains one hundred speakers on the rack and twenty separate switches on the table for each speaker in order to vary the communication locations. A third rack plus table registers the air consistency in every globe, the air pressure in five hundred locations. Any variation changes the color of the gauges. A fourth cluster of instruments holds the monitoring equipment and duplicate sets of display for the nuclear control room. It includes machinery rotation speeds, temperatures at various locations within the nuclear circuits, flow rate of the contained fluids, radiation levels and the power output in kilowatts.

The nerve center of the ISC is too confined in its vulnerability. Lee Powers proposed to build a duplicate set on the ISC. But the costs for such an installation seemed prohibitive to the board of the ISC's directors.

Lee Powers refers to Room 500 as the "Achilles' heel."

Kenny Andrews is in his late twenties. A scar runs across his dark West African features where a knife-wielding member of a juvenile gang left his mark. The injury shifts Kenny's nose slightly to the left, fixing his features in a perpetual snarl, an aspect which matches his tendency toward cruelty, but which also makes him curiously attractive to many women.

Sitting between his Chinese assistant Gay Chan and the Indian Indru, he manipulates switches on the control table, directing television lenses to zoom in for a close look on any activity that arouses his attention.

Ferranti turns off all sounds on his console. The images on the screens stay mute, like silent motion pictures.

Kenny watches Monitor 22. It shows five men in protective clothes, probing the seals of Reactor 1. They work with zombielike motions.

Kenny activates the sound and listens through headphones to muffled voices. The staccato click of Geiger counters rattles like a Morse code as the men seem to converge on the source of the radioactive spilling.

Kenny turns on Monitor 16, watching newly arrived

passengers inside the zerogravity train which takes them from the weightless atmosphere of the hangar toward the hotel's lobby. The television camera scans their faces; the microphone picks up a smattering of voices. With the sixth sense of a detective Kenny focuses the camera on two men, and the zoom lens depicts them in close scrutiny.

Activating the recorder of his control, Kenny marks the tape with his low, flat voice: "Astrocommuter flight eight oh three from New York. Check passenger list for man in gray sports coat, age about forty-five, bald, height about six feet, weight about one eighty, and man in blue serge, about thirty, weight one fifty plus. Men speak Slavic language." His voice contacts the security room, where Yamoto, his assistant, listens.

Indru switches his attention to Monitor 2, whose screen is parted in four segments, each showing a part of the outside controls. An astroferry hovers like a hummingbird near the hangar's closed door. It opens, and the ferry glides into the hangar.

Above the console a multitude of electronic eyes watch Kenny and his co-operators, transmitting their medical statuses, heart rates, temperatures, respiration rates, brain wave rhythms to the monitor room inside the ISC's hospital.

Gay Chan examines Monitor 34, which projects the hotel lobby. Passengers cluster around the reception desk, which is manned by a score of male and female clerks in the red uniforms of the Space Hotel. A bellboy soundlessly calls a passenger's name. The lobby is crowded like that of a grand hotel during a convention. Indirect lighting steals the shadows of the people, creating an eerie image of two-dimensional specters from another planet. The cupola of the hotel lobby is velvety dark, crisscrossed by thin laser beams threading a luminous red spider's web.

Gay bends sharply forward, focusing a zoom lens on the man in the gray sports coat and the younger one in blue. With singular determination the men walk up to a tall, aristocratic-looking, extremely thin passenger. His face with its high cheekbones and chiseled forehead looks cadaverous. His eyes, lying deeply in shadowy sockets, watch the approaching men apprehensively. He clutches an attaché case, chained to his left wrist, to his chest.

Suddenly the two men pounce on him. As Gay moves the zoom lens in to a close picture of the three, they become a whirling mass of limbs and heads. The cadaverous one is thrown to the floor, the thin one pulls at the chain fastened to the attaché case, the heavyset one is on top of the fighting, squirming heap, and as Gay turns on the microphone, screams of pain and shouting in a language Gay does not understand shriek from the loudspeaker in front of him. The passengers around the fighting men withdraw in surprise and shock.

"Trouble at reception," Gay announces, unruffled. Kenny wheels his chair around. His large black eyes, which never lose their feverish, nervous look, stare at the monitor. Background music from the hotel and a babble of voices, the sound of feet and a loudspeaker announcement fill the lobby. The announcer is not aware of the fight. "Astrocommuter to Sydney, Australia, leaving in ten minutes. Gate Three. Last call for Flight Three to Tokyo, Japan, and Sydney, Australia."

A circle has formed around the fighting group. Stunned by the incident, nobody comes to the fallen man's rescue. The heavyset man tries to yank the cadaverous one to his feet, shouting at him, but the man collapses like a rag doll, aware that he is safer lying down.

"Alarm red," Kenny says into the microphone

clipped to his shirt. His voice simultaneously returns from the lobby's loudspeaker. "Alarm red. Lobby. Reception."

Wearing olive-colored uniforms, three security guards appear as though materialized by Kenny's voice. The guards join the melee, parting the bodies. The two attackers are pulled off the man on the floor, who gets up, his face contorted with pain, blood dripping from his wrist where the chain has cut into his flesh. With his free hand he pulls a handkerchief from his breast pocket and pushes it between the chain and his wrist to arrest the bleeding.

A hush has fallen over the lobby. Muzak continues playing.

"You have no right to interfere." The bald-headed man tears himself loose from the guard. "We represent the People's Republic of Czechoslovakia. This man is an escaped convict."

"You have no jurisdiction on the ISC," Kenny's calm voice says over the loudspeaker. The man wheels around, searching for the source of the voice.

"He's carrying stolen money in that case. Our orders are to take him back with us!" he shouts. "I am acting on behalf of my sovereign country. That is, if that means anything up here."

"It doesn't," Kenny replies. "Please follow the guards to the security station, where you may file your complaint."

The Czech detective produces a pair of handcuffs and waves them over his head for the television cameras to see.

"I'm going to handcuff this man before he runs away," he announces defiantly.

"He cannot run anywhere. Please follow the guards," Kenny repeats patiently.

As the head of the ISC's security, Kenny protects the

satellite with intuition and foresight. He rarely leaves the monitor room in Globe 5. Watching the screen, he learns about the idiosyncrasies of its crew, its officers, scientists and guests. He records his observations in a computer on magnetic disks, a file which he keeps without anybody's knowledge. He even studies Lee Powers critically, aware of Lee's impatience, especially when a problem has been solved and a new one has not come up.

"I know you're a ruthless son of a bitch," Lee once told him. "That's no news to me. On the contrary, that's what prompted me to get you this job. I know you'll always live up to its demands. I'm also aware that you collect data about me. I don't mind that either. Good luck to you. I don't expect you to mellow, but you'd better stay within the written law of the ISC. The first trespass, and you're through. And I won't accept any explanation for whatever reason you thought the law had to be broken. Your dictionary is deficient. It doesn't contain the word 'ethics.' "

"I don't care about the means if they get results," Kenny said. "The security of this installation is more important than any personal consideration."

"Lawful consideration," Lee corrected him. "You've studied law; you were taught about right and wrong."

"Right and wrong are a matter of interpretation," Kenny answered. "I practiced my law in the streets, and I'm not sure mine doesn't work better than yours. The written law can't be applied to every situation. Laws are approximate; they have to be used when they bring results, not when they leave loopholes for a miscarriage of justice."

"Is that what you learned?" Lee asked.

"That's what circumstances and events taught me," Kenny said. "You can hit a man in such a way that he doesn't show bruises. I've still got that kind of invisible bruise."

"You'd better not let them control you, Kenny, or I'll have to fire you."

"Don't gloat too early," Kenny said, enjoying that slow ballet of minds between him and Lee. "I won't give you a chance to fire me."

A close relation exists between Lee and this young man. Kenny stole Lee's turbine car and was caught. Lee persuaded the judge to release the highly intelligent young black into his custody. He sent him through schools and colleges, training him for a job he had in mind and in which he needed a man he could trust implicitly: the head of the ISC's security force. The board of directors considered Kenneth Andrews much too young and inexperienced for this pivotal job, demanded a man twice his age, with experience in police work or the military. But Lee persuaded the board by accepting full responsibility for his choice.

On the monitor screen Kenny and Gay watch additional guards join the Czech detectives, leading them away. The cadaverous one follows his attackers. Like marionettes arrested in their motions, the passengers come to life, crowd the reception or walk on. The babble of voices rises again.

Ferranti turns off the sound in the monitor room.

"Did those two Czechs really believe they could drag a man into an astrocommuter and ship him back to Prague?" he says in a deliberate level voice, having trained himself never to show surprise.

"They must have hoped to intimidate us," Kenny answers, edgy and alert for danger. "Judge Nicopulos is going to lay down the law for them."

Nicopulos, a former judge of the International Court in the Hague, is judge and jury of the Space City.

On Monitor 26 a group of travelers appears. Kenny discovers Lee among them. At once he jumps up and crosses the room with two gigantic floating steps.

Room 500, the monitor center, is situated near the satellite's axis where the gravity pull diminishes.

"Just watch for me on the screens," he says hurriedly. "I'd better clear up that mess with those Czechs before Judge Nicopulos sends his report to Lee."

# IX

The spokes of the ISC's axis lead to Globe 10, where the hospital, the operating theater, the scientific and medical laboratories are located. Gravity 0.62 diminishes to 0.05. Every piece of equipment is secured to the walls and floor; the chairs and tables have magnetic tips on their legs to prevent them from floating but still making them ambulant. The hospital staff and the patients use electric carts, strapping themselves into the seats, or they walk with giant strides kept to the floor by magnetized shoes. Small batteries producing magnetism in the soles of the shoes hold them to the carpeting which has thin steel fibers woven into the fabric.

There are no beds in the hospital room where cases of severe burns are treated; the patients are suspended in midair, held in stationary position by thin strips of inflatable polymer. Broken bones are supported, without being encased, by narrow splints of the same material. In the rooms for decalcification a comfortable state of euphoria prevails under the constant gravity of 0.2. Ultra-low gravity depletes the calcium deposit in bones, a phenomenon discovered in astronauts and still not entirely explained. Strokes are forestalled by clearing cholesterol deposits from the blood vessels. Rooms 118 to 130 contain the beauty salons, the "Fountain of Youth" department. At gravity 0.05 muscles tighten the skin, lift jowls, breasts and stomachs. Tissues recover from the constant pull of earth's gravity, and stay in place. After a few weeks at the "Fountain," patients shed their aged looks without the assistance of a plastic surgeon.

Rooms 150 to 162 harbor the research laboratories, probing the effects of low gravity on moods and the delicate feedback of sensations. Rooms 80 to 117 are assigned to patients with coronary heart conditions. Gravity is constant at a comfortable 0.3; the heart uses only a tenth of its muscle power to pump blood.

Bodies become almost weightless; one has to watch out that a hand does not overshoot its mark when picking up an object. Patients have to be trained to avoid sudden movements; they must turn in slow motion, or they will revolve like unintentional acrobats.

Lee Powers and Ingmar Bergstrom, the Swedish chief surgeon, walk toward the coronary wing. Their movements are restrained, measured. A sudden thrust of an arm would wheel them around; too strong a step would catapult them to the tunnel's ceiling.

Lee critically observes the behavior pattern of his steps, studying the Coriolis effect on his body. The spinning of the spacecraft tries to veer his body diagonally, like a man walking on a merry-go-round.

"You cope well with the Coriolis; you can even walk in a straight line," he says to Bergstrom. "I have to adjust myself to the low-gravity zones every time I return from earth."

"I'm used to it," Bergstrom replies. "I wonder if I still can walk on earth. The last time I was there, I moved sideways like a crab." His studious, pale face, small and fragile under the weight of the enormous dome of a balding head, flickers a smile.

"How ill is McVeigh?" Lee asks.

"Very," Bergstrom grunts, showing his displeasure with his patient. "He insists on seeing you. And you'd better not upset him. He's the type that has perennial heart attacks. He should sit on his porch and stop scheming! Ambition is going to kill him."

"He must be close to seventy."

"Sixty-six. No age for a man of his constitution. He was sixty-four when he had that heavy thrombosis that crippled him for the rest of his Presidential term. He's had a few unpleasant flurries since. They were checked. And now he wants me to replace his heart with a plastic one. Atom-powered, of course. He might make it. He wants to live forever, it seems."

"But why?" Lee asks, politely but mechanically.

"I don't know," Bergstrom grumbles. "Most people want to live forever. What for? He had two terms as President. That job has no future, Powers. Where does a man go from there? But he wants the operation. Can I refuse him, a retired President of America? No!"

Lee's mind wanders off, probing important problems. The leak in Reactor 1 has been located; the cracked seal can be replaced. That will be Rubikov's job. Lee tries to dismiss the problem from his mind, but the insecurity which Rubikov has transferred to him lingers on. Lee is a sensitive antenna for people's vibrations; other people's moods stay with him, a shortcoming but also an asset. He is aware of Rubikov's deep, almost maniacal worries about the ISC.

Rubikov, brought up in a society which demands collective thinking, shows fissures as bad as that in Reactor 1. Lee's approach to problems doesn't conform with Rubikov's confined acceptance of ideas, those of a highly competent *aparatchik*, who does his duties reliably. He is unable to admit failure even to himself: His government would quickly replace him for any shortcoming. Lee tries to tell him that perfection is not possible on this intricate satellite, that the ISC is not fail-safe and never will be. But Rubikov believes that he is responsible for any mishap. He ingeniously and constantly improves every safety factor of his department. But luck cannot be regulated; a chain of unforeseen circumstances could bring disaster to the atomic power reactors and doom the satellite. Should Rubikov survive such a tragedy, he would find a way to blame himself.

Lee dismisses Rubikov's compulsive worries from

his mind and turns now to Bergstrom. "You put Tomlinson in the hospital. What's the matter with him?"

"How do you know he's in the hospital?" Bergstrom asks.

"Secrets are the seeds of difficulties," Lee says angrily, to hide his anxiety about his friend. "I don't want secrets between us, Bergstrom. Hell, tell me what's the matter with him!"

"Heart fibrillations. I should put him in the same bed with McVeigh. He should have his valves replaced. You talk to him. I wish he had some of McVeigh's will to live."

"What does McVeigh want from me?"

A few nurses and interns pass Lee and Bergstrom. Some walk in giant steps, lunging forward as if pushed by springs; others drive past in tiny carts, secured by seat belts. A well-dressed woman, pushing herself forward with both feet simultaneously like a kangaroo, smiles at Bergstrom.

"Don't I do all right, Doctor, with my new heart?" she calls out as she passes, her old face rapturously turned to Bergstrom.

"She was worse off than Tomlinson is now," Bergstrom says, looking after her. "Up here she's all right. We'll see how well she does when she gets back to earth, at gravity one."

"You didn't answer my question. Did McVeigh tell you why he wants to see me?"

"Not a word. When he was President, he left a hundred thousand papers behind stamped 'secret.' He hasn't changed; he won't confide in anyone. Though he might in you." Bergstrom shrugs. "Send me a Russian any day, not one of your 'kings for four years.' The Russians have the Politburo watching over their boys, afraid they might rear another Stalin. But your man has lost perspective on his own importance. If you ask me, he had too much power when he was in office.

I don't like one man having the finger on the button that can blow up the world."

Lee laughs. Bergstrom's gloominess amuses him.

"This is solely your department, Bergstrom. You don't have to operate on him. Throw him out. That's your prerogative."

"I know I should," Bergstrom grumbles. "But what about my medical ethics? I've been brainwashed by my profession. I'd like to send him and his bum heart home to his ranch in Delaware, but I have a conscience. Believe me, Powers, a conscience is a big drawback in life. McVeigh hasn't got one, or he wouldn't be trying to stay alive forever, which might well happen with that artificial heart I'm making for him. Why is he so eager? You find out."

The door in front of them slides back, and they enter the hospital.

# X

James L. McVeigh—L for Lavelle, his French ancestor from his mother's side—points the remote-control switch of his television set like a handgun at the screen covering the large wall opposite his bed in the ISC's hospital room. On the screen the earth slowly rotates. McVeigh studies the cloud formations over middle America, the swirl of a hurricane over the Virgin Islands, and comes to the conclusion that it is finally going to rain on his parched ranch in Delaware. A turn of the switch brings in other stations: a motion picture in French, a fashion show in Rome and a political rally in Washington, where a placard-bearing crowd demands less spending on armaments.

McVeigh turns off the monitor and slides down in his bed. His face shows the pallor, the veined bulbous nose of the cardiac patient. He closes his eyes, counting numbers, adding them at random, to take his attention off the picture in his mind. But he cannot shake it.

Nothing seems to have changed since the day a severe heart attack cut down his energies, almost terminating his life, and forced him to abandon the Presidency.

McVeigh had favored the military establishment; he had fed money and new powers to his military advisers, who played on his personal insecurities. Now, lying in a hospital bed with nothing to do but examine his life, he wonders if time is changing too drastically for him to comprehend. Can it be that those people on the television, clamoring for different values, might be right? The military machines still grind on, relentlessly, feeding data into computers, directing their policies according to the computer's decisions. Explosive forces equal to thirty tons of TNT for every human being on earth are stored up.

McVeigh has begun to feel guilty for his part in this madness. His predecessors started it, but he could have rechanneled the funding; he was in the position to direct them either way.

The International Space City is the Noah's Ark of his age. It is McVeigh's private ark. He supported Lee Powers' ideas, pushing them through the Ways and Means Committee, getting the allocations, not only from the House of Representatives and Senate, but also from foreign governments.

Space City! A symbol proving that all nations could work together if they have a common goal. If only men will come to believe in it!

But the ISC was never more than a symbol to the government on earth. Their goodwill was melting away, like icebergs in a warm ocean. Force was applied by guns and explosives.

McVeigh turns, half-asleep, and moans.

"Mr. President!"

The nurse shakes him. Her concerned young face bends over him.

"Don't wake me up, you silly cow. I was just falling asleep," McVeigh barks. "Why wake me up? To give me my sleeping pill?"

"You were having a nightmare," the nurse says and steps back. She is a dark-skinned girl from Liberia. At first she was awed and thrilled to be the former American President's nurse, but watching over the cranky, crude old man is causing her patience to wear thin.

"Nothing can happen to me, damn it," McVeigh grunts. "I've got more wires in me than the White House. I'm being monitored constantly, and you know it. I can't even fart without the doctors measuring it."

The girl covertly looks at her wristwatch. In one hour she will be released.

McVeigh closes his eyes again, glad that the nurse woke him from his painful dream. He recalls the night after his inauguration, when he lay elated in the bed which once supported Lincoln's long, bony frame. McVeigh is Lincoln's size, though more heavily built. Like every President before him, he thought of outshining all former leaders the world had produced—of becoming a giant figure, a man to stand beside Lincoln, Disraeli, Peter the Great and Churchill. When he was in office, he pushed himself more than his Cabinet and assistants. But his heart revolted. Now he is going to conquer that reluctant servant of his. He will have it replaced with a reliable one—as he used to replace people when he doubted their loyalty.

The furniture in the hospital room is made of plastic, poured in forms on earth, compressed before being taken into space, where, the pressure released, it expands into its original shape. The room looks antiseptic, monkish, despite its brightly colored plastic furniture, its light-green plastic walls, the Vycor window looking out upon the galaxy.

How much of the body can be exchanged by plastic parts? McVeigh ruminates. The heart, the kidneys, the arteries; what else? The skull, yes. But certainly not his brain. A chill runs through him. He does not want to die.

Bergstrom visits him twice every day. McVeigh somehow likes him but also resents him, since he cannot force his will on the surgeon.

"When Bergstrom comes in, you get out quick!" McVeigh says to the nurse. "Don't stick around like this morning."

Tightening the belt around her slim waist, the nurse gets up as the door opens and Lee, accompanied by Bergstrom, enters.

"You asked for me, Mr. President," Lee says.

"I did," McVeigh grumbles, "and you let me wait."

"I was in Switzerland," Lee says, aware that McVeigh is trying to put him on the defensive. Bergstrom motions the nurse to leave the room; then he steps closer to the bed.

"You shouldn't see anybody until you're in better physical shape," he says sternly, as he has trained himself to talk to obstinate patients. Being in constant fear of a failing heart leaves most patients with no psychological outlet except anger, and McVeigh, who once held the most powerful position on earth, all too obviously resents his weakened condition. "You can have five minutes with Mr. Powers. Not one minute more."

"You're abusing your position," McVeigh grunts. "I've used doctors only twice in my life, and both times they almost killed me."

"If you don't follow my orders, I can't take any responsibility for you." Bergstrom moves slowly toward the door and winks at Lee.

"What responsibility." McVeigh sneers, lifting himself up in bed. Since the gravity is low, he slides up easily. "If I kick off, on account of your quack treatment, who's going to blame you? Doctors have no responsibility toward their patients. Doctors are sacrosanct, untouchable. There's no chance blaming them for anything, except when they forget a scalpel in somebody's belly. I wish it were as easy in politics to hide mistakes. Ours are written up in history; yours just turn into bills."

His closely set eyes, glittering and sharply alive, study Lee. "Remember, Powers, how I got you the dough for your space project? I clubbed the English, Russians and French into coming up with a few billions. I must've had the premonition that I'd end up here with a bum heart."

Bergstrom closes the door behind him. Lee pulls a chair close to the bed. Its magnetic legs fasten to the floor.

"I'm glad the space hospital can do something for you, Mr. President." He has never liked this man, with his insecurities hidden behind a deliberate crudeness; he even used to drag his Cabinet to the bathroom with him, conducting discussions while he was sitting on the toilet. Every decision he made was for the judgment of history. Even his crudeness fits the pattern, making him more colorful in the eyes of historians. It is McVeigh's deliberate method to break a man down before he uses him. Lee is aware of it.

McVeigh bends forward, his hand cupping his large ear. "What did you say? Speak up, speak up."

Lee waits deliberately, then repeats in the same tone of voice, "I'm glad the hospital can do something for you."

"I can't hear what you're saying."

"You can. We have only five minutes. Shall we piss them away with pretenses?"

McVeigh glares at Lee.

"You wouldn't have dared talk to me like that when I was in the White House." A grin splits his face, revealing humor behind the mask. "I like you, Powers. You're not afraid of anything or anybody. I like men who do a lot and talk little. Most men don't have the intelligence to pour piss out of a boot. I remember when you told me you'd go ahead without our space industry, tying up with the Chinese and Russians, with the Europeans, even Albania!" He chuckles, and his jowls, flabby from having lost their fatty tissue, quiver. "Do you think I'll survive that butcher's knife?"

"If Bergstrom can't succeed, nobody can," Lee says. "But he doesn't want you exerting yourself. I'd stick to his rules. He's the guy with the know-how. Better trust him."

"I'll have to." McVeigh's mouth opens like that of a carp, and he gulps air. "I know how bad off I am. He doesn't even want me to think. Tell a man he shouldn't think of a pink elephant and he can't get that beast out of his mind! My mind starts walking its own road as soon as I close my eyes. I had a couple of cardiacs before, and I've trained myself to control my mind. Black it out. I can do it with yoga. But not in my dreams, and that quack doesn't want to give me tranquilizers or a sleeping pill. He says it's bad for the heart."

Lee waits for McVeigh to come to the point—why he asked for him. Rubikov is waiting to discuss the problem of the reactor, and Lee still has to see Tomlinson, to find out how he is doing: the interplanetary spacecraft he is going to test has arrived in its hangar. He has to check with Judge Nicopulos about the men who attacked their compatriot at reception.

"Bergstrom's put so many restrictions on me that I have to send for a nurse just to pick my nose," McVeigh complains. "You're the boss up here; I want you to act for me."

"I don't know what you're talking about," Lee says. "My authority is restricted. You're Bergstrom's patient."

"Nobody has ever fought me over such small items as that silly quack. I can't be here in bed indefinitely, pissing my time away. I want a direct communication system to my office in Delaware. He even refuses to let me talk on the videophone. He's cut off all my contacts with earth! He's quarantined me as if I had leprosy. My time is limited, Powers. I want you to okay my requests—God knows they're only reasonable. Get me a videophone, and get Bergstrom to let me have at least one visitor every day!"

"That's up to Bergstrom. If you want to forgo that operation, you won't be under his orders. So as long as you want to go through with it, he's the boss. Sorry."

Lee resents this man's wasting his time.

"Bergstrom is overreacting," McVeigh complains. "Just because I held that government position for a few years. I need a communication center right here in this room. I must continue my preparations for the future." His voice rises in his excitement.

"You're in just the state of mind Bergstrom is trying to prevent," Lee says. "Excitement is not healthy for you."

McVeigh probes at Lee with his hypnotic eyes.

"All right, you want me to speak bluntly. But I can't stand people blabbering about things that are important to me. So keep your mouth shut. I want to run for President again."

Lee blinks in surprise, looking at McVeigh's pale, wasted face.

"Doesn't the Constitution permit only two terms, Mr. President?"

"I know, the Twenty-second Amendment." McVeigh's tiny eyes become mischievous slits. "Let me worry about that! There'll be a powerful motion in the Senate and the House to change that based on the merit of the man who has served his country well. A new amendment will permit a former President to run again after a hiatus of eight years. A governor has that right; why not the President? Bergstrom says I could live a hundred more years. My mind hasn't gone dotty, and I don't think it ever will. There's nothing wrong with my body except that skippy heart, and that'll soon be an atom-powered mechanical plant. But in the meantime I must be kept informed what's going on. I've made mistakes, but a clever man makes his mistakes only once. My public relations people have worked out a new image for me: a man whose heart can't be damaged." He starts to laugh, but a spasm of coughing stops him. He fights for air.

"Now you know what I have in mind. That operation is just an incidental thing; it's mechanical, a butcher's job. I'm being rewired, that's all. What's important is up here." He taps his head. "I'm going to be a better President, since I've had more than a full term of experience. So don't you see—I can't let myself be stymied by a surgeon who has no regard for his patient. I'm just a number to Bergstrom; he has more sympathy for his laboratory rats than for me." His face loses the tense, guarded look. His eyes turn introspective.

Lee realizes the power this crafty man still wields. He probably has the idea of holding office again for many years.

"You know, Powers, when I ran the country, I didn't do a bad job, I must say. History will give me an A plus for all the good things I did for the people. I have compassion for them. But I don't think they've given me the credit I'm due. Why not?"

Lee shrugs. "You're not a likable man." The fathomless ego of this man, still powerful even when lying half-dead in an intensive care room, makes Lee uncomfortable.

"You tell Bergstrom that I need a videophone. I must stay in touch with certain people to get the amendment through. Bergstrom has no right to stand in the way of history. And by the way, I want another nurse. That black bitch depresses me."

Bergstrom enters, with a lifted left wrist, looking at his watch.

"Time's up," he announces. "I gave you one more minute than I should. Powers, out with you!"

Lee at once gets up, relieved to get away from the cranky, scheming man.

"My jailor!" McVeigh exclaims, but grinning at Bergstrom with an engaging grin, an echo of the charm he used when he was President. "When will my time be up?"

"In a few days you'll be better than new," Bergstrom promises.

# XI

"I discussed that problem with Vera Stern," Behrmann says, his moon face showing the shrewd, calculating expression of a chess player who has figured out an intricate move. "We came to the conclusion that I'll have to operate on every one of you, without delay."

The committee meets in the commissary, which Miranda has again searched for hidden listening devices.

The men and women around the table show an alertness which is in contrast with their former veiled despair.

"Surgery," Ibbotson repeats, twisting his mouth. "You want to remove that gabby monitoring device, our Adam's rib!"

"You're using a male chauvinistic simile," Cypriana says with a breathless, jagged laugh. "You're comparing the monitoring device with a female, just because it's something mean, base, nasty, soulless, wretched, vile!"

Her dislike for the burly man expresses itself in a hard, disgusted stare. Bardou suspects that her attack on Ibbotson stems from a former relation which she now finds distasteful.

She is sitting close to Bardou, not having left him since his arrival. She spends her nights in his room, replenishing her strength by being near him.

The first night they were together, Bardou said, "You made me vulnerable, Cypriana."

"Why?" she questioned gaily, embracing him more tightly. "Am I too young for you? I wasn't aware of it the last few hours. Or are you afraid of falling in love with me, a girl your daughter's age? That'd be a novel sensation for you, wouldn't it?"

Her observation fell on him like a blow.

"I know that our age difference doesn't mean anything to you or to me. But we're not in Paris or Manila where a girl can visit her lover in secret. You're young; you haven't developed the calloused stamina I have. So far I've only had myself to contend with. If our plan fails, I die alone. But now you've become my responsibility. That's what makes me feel vulnerable."

"You can't share death; everybody dies alone," she said soberly. "But what you just said proves that you love me."

"Would it make things easier for you if I were in love with you?" he asked, and felt a heavy excitement rising between him and the girl. She leaned her face so close to him that he felt her breath.

"It would make me feel less lonely," she said gently. "We're like two people on a ship in a storm. I'd like to tie us together with a rope, to be found together should we die. Having me so close to you should make you stronger and less vulnerable. Being alone was like death to me. Now I'm alive. Did you watch those faces change at the committee meeting? They were acting like zombies, but you brought them back to life."

He was silent, and in his silence there was understanding and trust.

"It wouldn't be a great hardship spending the rest of my life with you up here," he said quietly.

"Do I remind you of someone you once knew?" she asked, jealous of a phantom.

"No; you're the only Cypriana I've ever met."

Her lips close to his ear, she whispered, "You're going to succeed. I know you will, because your desires are my prayers."

"To succeed isn't up to me alone!"

It seemed to him that time, which he thought had

stopped, suddenly was passing by feverishly. "We haven't told the plan to our fellow prisoners. How many would risk their lives on a chance with such low odds of succeeding?"

"They'll do whatever you tell them," she said confidently, stroking the skin of his forehead to smooth out the worry lines. "Just consider me a result of a poll. Didn't I do a hundred percent what you asked of me? You can do the same with them. No, not quite the same"—she laughed mischievously—"that would make me jealous, and jealousy is against the law on the SP."

She kissed him, and Bardou forgot that he was floating in a space capsule five hundred miles above the earth, in a prison whose bars were made of vacuum.

Vera Stern's level and matter-of-fact voice brings him back to reality. She talks as if the space conspiracy were a routine action.

"Some of the implanted devices might stop functioning during or after their removal from the body. If they discontinue registering on Ground's monitors, Ground certainly will start an inquiry. We must keep the devices in constant working order. Dr. Behrmann and I suggest that each of the inmates carry the device with him all the time after removal, until the moment of departure."

"I'll contact Ground and tell them we have an epidemic of something," Ibbotson says. "We'll think of a good one. That's the time to leave the gadgets behind. They'll think everybody up here is sick in bed." He adds, "I'm in touch with Ground every day."

"That's what I want to change," Bardou says, giving vent to a suspicion. "From now on nobody should be permitted to contact Ground except in the presence of another member of the committee."

Ibbotson bridles.

"Are you implying that I can't be trusted?"

"I got the impression that nobody up here trusts anybody else. You told me yourself that some of the inmates spied for Ground or tried to make deals sacrificing their fellow prisoners. To give our plan away to Ground would be a powerful bargaining point, wouldn't it?"

"When we lived on earth, we had grandiose ideas how the world should be run," Miranda says with an apelike smile. "As it turns out, we can't even run this prison without being at each other's throats." He stares at Cypriana's eyes but cannot find a center in them. "Whom can we trust? Any two people could make a deal between them, couldn't they? What would stop them selling the rest of us out?"

"I need Cypriana in the radio room," Bardou decides.

"Ah!" Miranda's shoulders are hunched over the table. "You want to get that girl out of circulation and make sure where you can find her when you want her." He draws anger out of himself to cover his jealousy.

Behrmann watches Miranda with clinical interest.

"It would be a sound idea to have you castrated, Miranda. That'd change your disposition."

"You don't have to do anything to him," Cypriana says with casual cruelty, looking directly at Miranda. "What's left of his sex urge are wish dreams; the radiation has dried up the rest. If Pierre tells me to stay in the radio room, that's what I'll have to do. He's making the decisions."

"I don't trust her either," Miranda says. "Why shouldn't she trade information for freedom? That pregnancy scheme doesn't work with her. She's as barren as space itself."

Bardou hits the table with both fists, unable to control his fear that his carefully thought-out plan might be sabotaged by one of the conniving people around him.

"Have all of you gone crazy? From now on I'm going to decide about every step of this action. You can make suggestions and contribute your technical knowledge. No more! If that is agreed upon, I'll go on; otherwise I'm getting out of this game."

He eyes the group tensely.

"Who doesn't agree had better speak up now," he adds.

"I'm with you, Bardou." Hallstadt raises his hands in surrender. "Maybe we're all more or less mad. Who knows? I believe that you're still the sanest among us."

"All right." Bardou turns to Behrmann. "How many operations can you perform a day?"

"At least twenty. It needs only a small incision. The patient will have to stay in his room for a day or two. But to keep the devices working needs technical know-how."

"I have a few in the laboratory that need repair. Dr. Behrmann removed them from deceased prisoners," Mrs. Stern says. There is something inhuman and distant about her, as if her fellow inmates were only objects for her experiments. "I'll repair them, and we can use them as soon as onc of the removed ones fails. Then Ground won't become suspicious."

"Who's going to operate on Dr. Behrmann?" Kentu asks.

"I once removed my own appendix; I can do this one myself," Behrmann answers with a small smirk. "Cypriana will assist me. She's going to watch sixty removal operations; that'll make her quite efficient. If I die on the table, just report that you have a vacancy to fill."

Bardou looks at his notes. "Who can pilot a space ferry?"

"None of us," Hallstadt replies. "But we can persuade the pilot who brings up the astroferry with the weekly provisions to take us to the ISC."

"He's going to refuse," Kentu predicts.

"How could he?" Hallstadt answers quickly. "We'll tell him we're going to push him out the space lock."

"I think he'll see our point," Guzmán agrees. "But he might only pretend to cooperate, and fly us to Ground instead."

"He wouldn't, and couldn't," Vera Stern says impatiently. "The ferry is directed by preset computer. Besides, the pilot would have the perfect alibi that he was acting under the threat of death. He's being hired to fly for the ISC, not to die for it."

"How can we think of everything!" Ibbotson runs his large hands over his face in sudden despair.

"You baffle me," Hallstadt says. "You don't agree with Bardou's plan. Why sit in with us? Have you changed your mind, or do you want to sabotage us?"

"I'm still against it, but it's my duty to warn you of possible failures. I'm still head of the committee. I am entitled to my say!"

"We have nothing against you," Bardou answers calmly. "We welcome criticism as long as it's constructive. But we don't need you to tell us that we can't succeed. We have a collection of excellent minds on the SP. We won't lose that game."

Again he scans the faces surrounding him. How much pressure can those warped people endure before becoming completely unstable?

Calmly he reads off the next question: "How often does the ISC pass the SP?"

"I recorded the flight pattern of the ISC for the last two years," Miranda says. "Not only the ISC, but also satellites like the Australian and Japanese space labs. The ISC passes the SP every three hours and thirty-nine minutes."

"José and I diagnosed this problem," Vera Stern says.

Miranda, his corn-husk-colored face looking aged in concentration, produces loose sheets from his pocket.

"We checked out the necessary speed variations on the computer. The attacking ferry has to make a velocity change of twelve hundred and twenty-six feet per second to get into the path of the ISC."

"Speed, velocity," Bardou repeats with a blank look. "Isn't that the same?"

Miranda produces a snorting, contemptuous noise. "Go back to class! Speed indicates how fast a body is going; velocity tells about speed plus direction. Get it?"

"Thanks for the information, but do we have to know those details?" Bardou feels his pulse quicken in a sudden surge of annoyance. Miranda was carving out a position for himself by showing off his knowledge. "All right, go on, I'm learning fast."

"I've put the instructions on paper in case I'm not round when the escape ferry's computer has to be programmed. A few of the inmates also would know how to do it. I conducted a training program during the last year." Seeing Bardou's look of surprise and slight confusion, Miranda raises his voice in anger. "One has to do something on this mental wasteland, Bardou. Three came to listen. No more! Those three now have a basic knowledge."

"Why don't you call them in on this discussion?" Bardou asks.

"Because I want to teach you," Miranda shouts, his voice breaking in a shrill falsetto. "You said you want to be in charge. You'd better know what has to be done."

"Calm down, Miranda," Guzmán says in a flat, authoritative voice. "We know how important you are for us. Just tell us quietly."

Miranda gulps. His shoulders lifted, he stares at the notes in his hands. "To meet the ISC when it is closest to us, the ferry has to reach a speed of twelve hundred and twenty-six feet per second. Don't forget to program the computer for exactly twelve hundred and twenty-six feet speed gain, or you'll never reach the ISC—or you'll overshoot it. When the ferry is twelve miles away from the ISC, it must drop down to exactly two hundred and fifty feet speed per second. Understand? I wrote the information down in precise detail."

"Wouldn't we depend on the ferry's pilot?" Bardou asks, worried by Miranda's quickly changing moods. "If he sets the computer differently, he could abort our plan."

"You were a professor of semantics," Miranda says scornfully. "You'd be a bust in the department of physics. Of course I'm going to program the tape in advance. A tape which we just insert in the ferry's computer."

"Then why this discussion? I herewith appoint you to prepare that tape, which will be your sole responsibility," Bardou says quietly. "You can't expect us laymen to understand your business."

Miranda suddenly betrays an inner nervousness which his brashness has been covering. "I might die tonight, and somebody else has to know what to do."

"I hope you won't die," Vera says with veiled sarcasm, pushing Miranda aside with words. "We pass the node where we meet the ISC every two hundred and nineteen minutes. That means that about every three and a half hours we make our closest approach to the ISC."

As if to verify her statement, the ISC's musical approach comes softly from the radio, faintly, gaining in strength. "We'll meet the ISC over the Pacific. There the observation from the earth is the worst. When you hear this sound full strength"—Vera nods toward the radio, which is a small transistor hanging from the wall—"she is passing us. The ISC is not being watched as closely from Ground as in the beginning. Nor are we here on the SP—I'm sure that during the three years we've been up here we've become routine for Ground."

"We'll have to board the ferry thirty minutes before the propulsion is turned on." Sensing Bardou's aversion to him, Miranda turns to him. "Sorry I shouted at you, Bardou. But when you've been caged in up here for two years as I have, damn it, you don't control your nerves all the time; they sometimes control you."

As he apologizes to Bardou, he glances at Cypriana.

"Even if we should miss the ISC at the precise moment, there's another chance coming up every three hours and thirty-nine minutes," Guzmán says, a haggard look on his round face.

"What are you going to do when you succeed in boarding the ISC?" Ibbotson asks, as though the spacejacking were Bardou's private undertaking.

"Yes, exactly what's your plan?" Behrmann asks, his round eyes watching Bardou as if he were a patient with an unknown disease.

"That problem has been worked out." Bardou's eyes seek Cypriana's. He discovers a warning in them and quickly checks himself. "You'll find out in due time."

"We won't accept that uncertainty." Ibbotson's faded blue eyes glare at Bardou in ill-concealed hatred. "You can start a war easily—but can you finish it? So you occupy the ISC. They won't take that lying down. There are three thousand people against you. Armed security guards. You don't know what kind of weapons they might use. Even if you get to the control room and are able to paralyze the ISC—what then? What then?"

"If you know the answer, why keep it from us?"

Guzmán joins in. "Do you want us to risk our lives without knowing what we're doing?"

"I'm going to put my instructions on paper as soon as we're through with this meeting. I hope I won't die in the meantime."

Bardou again glances at Cypriana for her reaction and discovers relief in her face. Quietly she gets up and leaves the room.

Hallstadt leans back calmly, eyeing the group with a languid, cynical amusement. For him the conference is just like any plan of attack on an unsuspecting town. He has been through situations of this kind before, but none in which the participants mistrust each other more than the enemy.

"Doesn't all this seem to you like a game we're playing to pass the time?" he asks in a bored manner. "How can we ever succeed if we don't trust each other?"

Bardou deliberately ignores him.

"There must be some of our inmates who've been to the ISC and know its layout."

"I was at the hospital on the day of its inauguration," Behrmann says. "The hospital is situated in Globe Ten in the middle axis, near the control room."

"The nerve center!" Shepilov joins the discussion. "I was permitted to visit the ISC as the literary representative of the Russian government. Their layout is very similar to our satellite. If we reach the center without being stopped, all we have to do is cut a few cables or sabotage a few computers. That would upset the whole ISC system."

"We do have people on the SP who've been to the ISC," Ibbotson says, suddenly cooperative. He turns cumbersomely in the swivel chair, wracked by painful arthritis and short of breath because of emphysema. The pressure of the conference seems to have aggravated his condition. "Let me find them. They might be helpful." Softly and in slow motion, he moves out of the commissary.

Hallstadt lifts his hand as if holding a glass to toast the group.

"We have the advantage which almost guarantees success. The first law to victory is to surprise the enemy. Get him off-balance! If we can hold the control room, the ISC becomes a space prison and we are the jailors!"

"I suggest we call a general meeting of everybody on the SP," Bardou decides. "We'll explain our plan and take a vote."

"On what?" Van Buren asks, startled.

"Not everyone might be in favor of the spacejacking," Bardou says. "Some might think they're signing their death warrant. They might prefer to stay."

"I certainly will," Vera Stern says suddenly, and the committee members stare at her in surprise.

"But we need you!" Behrmann says.

The woman shakes her head. "You need me here. I'll be your safeguard. You can threaten Ground that in case they refuse to give you amnesty, I could blow up the reactor compartments and radioactive debris would scatter through space. That would endanger the ISC's orbit area, and cause radioactive parts to fall to earth. It would certainly damage the ISC and kill or seriously injure its inhabitants. A fallout of that kind would be a disaster to earth. There are many important people on the ISC; I don't think Ground would dare endanger their lives. This is your major trump in dealing with Ground."

"If we can do that," Kentu says, suddenly coming to life, "why attack the ISC at all? Just threaten Ground that we will destroy the SP, and that would be enough pressure on them to deal with us and to proclaim a general amnesty."

"No," Bardou replies dryly. "I've thought of that possibility, too. The negotiations would drag on, even if we set a time limit. Ground would deliberately prolong the conferences and in the meantime evacuate the ISC completely."

"And jeopardize its investment? Don't be ridiculous!" Shepilov says. "We aren't worth three hundred billion dollars to them!"

"Ground will need a unanimous decision from all the nations that contributed. Some might not go along; there's never been a perfect agreement in the United Nations as long as it's existed," Bardou says.

"We have no explosives," Shepilov remarks. "How could the ISC be blown up?"

"Ground can't be sure of that," Hallstadt answers. "In warfare bluff often succeeds. The U.S. had only two atom bombs in World War II, but the Japanese didn't know that. The U.S. dropped those two on Hiroshima and Nagasaki, and Japan came to terms."

"Hans can work out a method," Van Buren says, confident of his friend's abilities in weaponry. "If we die, Vera and the people left behind have no chance either. If we succeed, they too will be free."

"I'm going to stay here to the end of my days," Vera Stern announces. "I'll be the safeguard that you're not double-crossed on earth. Besides, I'm perfectly happy in my lab and away from the turmoil down below."

She stops. A woman's voice screams high and wild like a cat's. Bardou and Hallstadt jump up and race to the door. Hallstadt, used to the low gravity, shoots ahead of Bardou as though he had wings, toward the room from which the shouts of pain emerge.

Bardou tries to stop the inertia of his floating by holding onto the frame of Ibbotson's office door. Inside the room Hallstadt descends on two bodies which bounce clumsily up and down. Cypriana claws at Ibbotson's face, and the heavy man is hitting her with both fists. Her face is bloodstained, contorted in fury, her wide open mouth spurting blood. Suddenly the room is crowded with people; the room reverberates with shouts of anguish and fury. Bardou reaches Cypriana and pulls her away from Ibbotson's grip. She pushes him away with unexpected strength, her eyes filled with hatred, fastened on Ibbotson's bleeding face.

"He tried to contact Ground to give us away!" she screams and again leaps on Ibbotson, who is held back by Hallstadt and a man with a pockmarked face.

"I didn't!" Ibbotson shouts back at her, vainly trying to free himself. His body shakes in a sudden abysmal fear, and his voice drops to a whisper. "Believe me, I didn't!"

"That bastard!" Van Buren is in the room, near the videophone. "See, he punched the Ground buttons, fortunately not all of them. He tried to contact Ground."

"I didn't!" Ibbotson tries to turn around in the grip of Hallstadt and the other man. "She jumped me out of nowhere. I don't know why."

"I knew he'd try to betray us!" Cyprina screams. In her fury she tries again to claw at Ibbotson's face. Bardou puts his arms around her and pulls her away. Her soft body against his, she suddenly collapses and starts to cry. "I knew it, I knew it all the time!"

"She's lying!" Ibbotson shouts. Van Buren hits his neck with a vicious chop. Half-numbed, Ibbotson tries to turn, but Hallstadt pulls him toward the door like a rag doll.

"Don't!" Bardou shouts, anticipating Hallstadt's intent. "We must find out what happened; we must have a trial."

"It's clear to me!" Van Buren, at the door, pushes Ibbotson's half-floating body. "It's clear to everybody what he tried to do."

Bodies, pulling and tearing at Ibbotson, disappear from Bardou's view. He is still holding Cypriana, who clings to him with blind need.

"It's no use," she whispers, her voice breaking. "He's guilty. You can't stop them."

# XII

The interplanetary spacecraft XC-17 has been assembled in the hangar adjoining Globe 5. Its oval body extends spidery tentacles, each ending in an odd-shaped disk. Lee Powers walks around the huge beetlelike contraption like a jockey critically eyeing a horse he is going to ride.

"Are you going with us to Mercury?" asks a man with a smooth Oriental face, dressed in a peach-colored overall. His young, unlined features are as calm as that of a benign temple figure.

"You might have the pleasure of my company," Lee mutters. Three men, the crew of the XC-17, are climbing over the spacecraft, testing it with radioactive beams for hidden faults in the material.

"You designed it, Dr. Powers. I'm sure its fail-safe," the young Oriental says in awe.

"If we return, it is," Lee answers offhandedly. "To fly that thing is the real job, not to design it. I just followed established pattern."

Gerald Tomlinson, leaning on a walking stick, watches Lee disapprovingly. His face is pasty, his heavy body bloated by the water which his weak heart cannot shed.

Half-floating in diminished gravity, Lee circles the XC-17 in giant strides, jumping high to touch its shimmering skin. The young co-pilot imitates his movements.

"We're honored having you on the trip," the co-pilot says, bowing gracefully in midair.

"Really?" Lee turns to him with an ironic smile. "Don't I take some of your glamor away?"

"Having fun?" Tomlinson asks in his gravel voice.

Lee shifts his direction by a quick jerk of his head to

face his friend. The pilot jumps backward away from him to leave the two men alone.

"I didn't know you were here. Does Bergstrom permit this foolishness of getting out of bed?"

"If I followed the advice of doctors, I'd have been dead long ago. Bergstrom even told me to give up my six o'clock martini."

"It's six o'clock every fourteen minutes," Lee says, and laughs.

The old man takes a long, careful step that floats him close to Lee.

"I don't approve of your taking that contraption into space," he says in a low, worried voice. "Leave the acrobatics to the space jockeys, to people who've been training for months to man this thing. Why take risks? What do you want to prove?"

"We always want to prove the same thing, over and over again, don't we, Jerry?" Lee answers indulgently. He presses a button on the craft's belly and a thin ladder unfolds. At its top a door slides back. "We want to show ourselves we're still alive. Come on, let's have a look inside."

"Do you doubt that you're alive? You want to risk your life to challenge fate?"

"Crap!" Lee snaps. "Drop that father image; I'm old enough to make my own decisions." He stretches out his hand, and Tomlinson takes it. Their bodies almost weightless, they ascend the ladder.

"You're like that alcoholic who shouldn't drink but goes to a bar and orders a triple whiskey," Tomlinson says. "He gulps it down and convinces himself that he has been stronger than his willpower."

"You're full of stories with no relation to anything you want to say." Lee steps inside the XC-17's body. Instruments and small windows of computers cover one wall. There are four seats facing the control panel.

Lee reaches one with a carefully timed step and sits down, fastening a seat belt.

"I like to be the first one in an unknown venture," he says.

"I know, I know!" Tomlinson says wearily, sitting beside him. "Your concern about your own importance will finally break your neck. To be the first in everything! Why? What's driving you? They sent spacecraft to Mercury, orbited Venus and Jupiter, photographed its moons. Others are on their way to farther planets. But those are instrumented, unmanned spacecraft, my dear boy."

"But men landed on Mars without me," Lee complains. "Just because I was busy with this space hotel, the haven for the ultrarich, the idle, the parasites." He moves his face closer to Tomlinson's. "But the XC-seventeen is going to land on Mercury! We'll land on its shady side and spend several weeks before it rotates to face the sun again."

"And if you don't get off the ground in time? You'll just shrivel up, burned by the surface heat."

Lee caresses the instrument board in front of him.

"I worked on the construction of the XC-17. This craft is safe. The thermal heat shield protects the ship and the crew from the sun until it's close enough to get into the shadow of the planet. Can you imagine what it means being the first human being to set foot on a new planet?"

Tomlinson sits tight-lipped and silent until Lee finishes his exuberant outburst.

"We have enough unmanned spacecraft which can do all the necessary configurations. Why go to Mercury if we already have the information?"

"You can't program a computer for everything. To get knowledge needs judgment, reasoning, perception and the infinite choice of decision that only a human brain can produce. A computer can't react to unforeseen circumstances; only a man can make multiple choices and return with precise information."

Tomlinson stares hard at Lee. "What's the matter with you?" he finally asks. "When will you stop playing Buck Rogers?"

"The Sunday sermon again!" Lee shakes his head. "What's wrong with spending a few months of my life exploring? I won't be alone; I'll have an excellent crew along with me. I won't do anything more dangerous than those men."

Tomlinson watches him, unmoved. "Go on," he says.

"Go on with what?"

"Why are you so bored with yourself?" Tomlinson asks. "You've made the encyclopedias, so your reason can't be ambition. I visualize you being cooped up for months in the XC-Seventeen, watching computers perform. Then landing on some damned planet, collecting rocks and air samples, if there is any air. Returning from a trip that takes months of boredom. Of course, arriving a hero! So what? You know what we're doing with our lives? We replace what we've used up, that's all. You've used up the excitement that comes from outside influences, like building the City in the Sky. Whatever you do from now on will be repetitious. You won't find anything really new on Mercury."

Lee surveys Tomlinson sullenly.

"I feel useless," he finally confesses. "The ISC doesn't need me. I'm no administrator. I never will be a good one."

"Then why did you accept that job?"

"I've written to the board offering my resignation."

"Very good!" Tomlinson exclaims. "When did you mail the letter?"

"I wanted you to see it before I send it in," Lee confesses, lowering his voice. "I wouldn't take that step without informing you first. But I can't do anything up here that's of any value. The ISC runs by itself. I can't think of anything that could happen to it, except a collision with a giant meteor. And that's a chance of a billion to one. Besides, I couldn't do anything about it. I've decided to quit, Jerry." He closes his mouth hard, watching Tomlinson for a reaction. "How can I make myself clear? I don't care about the ISC anymore. It's behind me, an accomplished fact. I'm wasting my time up here. I'm going to take the XC-Seventeen on a test run, and if that run comes out all right, I'll take her up to Mercury."

"And after your return, what?" Tomlinson asks.

"I don't know yet. But before that question comes up, I'll have had a few months to do something worthwhile. I'm vegetating, Jerry. When there's a brawl between hotel guests, they call me to talk to the judge; when there's trouble with a reactor, I have to come up to hold Rubikov's hand. If a toilet breaks on the ISC, they call me. I can't take it any longer!"

"I'll never know what possesses you," Tomlinson says sadly. "Maybe if you had a few scrapes with death, you'd learn how important it is to be alive. Life is a shadow's dream, no more!"

"There you go again." Lee pats the older man's shoulder. "Quotations. And the wrong one!"

"I wish I were in good physical shape and thirty years younger—I'd come with you."

"Glad you understand me," Lee says with a sigh of relief.

"I do and I don't," Tomlinson answers softly. "All right, send your resignation to the board. I'll second you."

"Now you've come back to your senses!" Lee grins at him; then his face sobers. "It's strange that I need your approval for anything I do."

# XIII

The sightless shell turns its giant ear toward the sky. It traces radio vibrations from the Space Prison, moving with minute coordination, pinpointing the satellite until it dips beneath the horizon.

In the control room three hundred feet away from the round disk, the engineer on duty, Don Frazer, watches a bank of monitors. One of them shows on its opaque screen tiny light dots which move like illuminated ants. They are the reflections of the tracing devices the prisoners are forced to wear inside their bodies. Their movements are jerky, seemingly senseless.

Frazer has been on duty for almost eight hours. Soon the next shift will take over the watch. Frazer has become almost as inanimate as the radio telescope; only his sight is active, observing the dots for any unusual behavior.

He works four days continuously and has two days off, which become his Saturday and Sunday. They sometimes fall on a Tuesday or any other day of the week, since his week has six days, not seven.

Outside the control building the traffic of Menlo Park moves with muffled noises, oblivious to the presence of the enormous disk. Dozens of other radio telescopes are scattered all over the globe to monitor the SP: Goldstone in Arizona, Greenwich near London, Vevey near Geneva in Switzerland. Some others are strewn over India, Australia, Siberia. All are in contact with Ground in Brussels on a hot line, an instant videophone contact.

For three years the SP has passed over Menlo Park's radio telescope without incident. The soundless dots move and crawl without a set pattern. Frazer's eyes throw routine glances at the screen. He has almost forgotten what he is looking for during the ten minutes the satellite crosses the radio telescope's field of vision.

Frazer was in his early twenties when he was offered the job; he accepted it as a stopgap employment which would give him time to study for a master's degree and he hoped, a future PhD in astronomy. He intended at first to stay only a few months, but his complaisant job has dragged out for three years. By now he has become part of the electronic robot he serves.

Tonight Frazer's senses suddenly sharpen. He bends his lean body forward toward the monitor's screen and squints. The dots on the screen have stopped their movement, except for a few which carry on their slow routine.

Quickly Frazer punches a series of numbers on the videophone which connects him with Ground.

Ground is located in Brussels, at the Avenue Antwerp. Henri Lefrèvre is the engineer in charge. He watches a bank of videophones, each labeled with the location of a radio telescope.

Lefrèvre has been with Ground since its inception ten years ago. He intends to write a book about it, using copious notes which record his daily routine.

Tonight something mysterious and unexpected finally happens. Lefrèvre reacts sharply to the flashing light from Menlo Park, which is followed by continuous signals from radio telescopes all over the world.

Calmly and precisely Lefrèvre activates all screens. Faces appear on them: Frazer's in Menlo Park, Mandez's in Punta Arenas, Rimsky's in Tashkent and a dozen others.

"The transmissions from the SP have become static," Frazer reports. His usually complacent face is alive with excitement.

"Most tracing devices have stopped moving," Mandez adds. He and Frazer can see and hear each other.

"*Most* tracing devices?" Lefrèvre repeats, turning to the video screen with Rimsky's face on it. "How many?"

"Of the sixty, only four are active," Rimsky reports. "Something's going on on the SP. Can it be a transmitting failure?"

Lefrèvre does not reply. The observers are paid to watch, not to ask questions.

"Thank you," he says curtly. He darkens the screens, returning Frazer and the rest of the operators to their anonymous vigil.

He contacts Ground's headquarters in Geneva. The clock shows five minutes past two in the morning. The operator on duty answers.

"Get Signor Mancini for me," Lefrèvre tells the sleepy night operator.

"Signor Mancini went home for the weekend," the operator reports. Mancini is the present head of Ground.

"Connect me with him," Lefrèvre demands impatiently.

"He told me not to disturb him," the operator objects. "Only in emergencies."

"This *is* an emergency!" Lefrèvre can barely control his annoyance.

Mancini's sleep-drugged face appears on Lefrèvre's monitor screen.

"This is a hell of a time to get a man out of bed," he grumbles. "What's the rush?"

"Something's happening up at the Space Prison," Lefrèvre says, his voice officious and steady. "The prisoners have stopped moving about."

"They have what?" Mancini asks, trying to shake his head clear of sleep.

"The radio telescopes all over the world report a sudden stop of activities on the SP."

Mancini fights his numbed brain. He has taken two Seconal tablets, which dull his thinking process.

"Get in touch with the SP," he forces himself to say. His tongue weighs heavily in his mouth. "Find out what's the matter. Report back to me. But not before ten in the morning, all right?"

"I understand," Lefrèvre says. He knows the old man from previous encounters. There should be an age limit for the position as chairman of Ground, he decides. Sixty should be the limit; then younger people should take over. Lefrèvre is forty-eight.

"Thank you, Henri," Mancini says, his eyelids made of tin, "I'm sure it has a simple explanation. What could happen up there?"

"The inmates might have died!"

"Well, that wouldn't make much difference. A life sentence or death is pretty much the same. I'd prefer the latter."

The light disappears and leaves an empty screen.

Lefrèvre feels a sudden surge of pride and anticipation. Mancini has entrusted him with a great responsibility. If he handles the SP matter cleverly, he might advance to a higher position—might even, one day, become chairman of Ground.

A direct line connects Ground with the Space Prison. Relayed over radio telescopes, it contacts the SP even when it passes the opposite side of the globe, the Marquesas Islands.

Lefrèvre calls the SP. But instead of the bearded Ibbotson's face, that of a young woman appears on the screen.

"This is Ground," Lefrèvre says. "Who are you?"

"Cypriana Maglaya."

Lefrèvre studies her thin, smooth-skinned features, her slanted eyes, and tries to remember the girl and her crime.

"Let me talk to Stig Ibbotson."

"He's ill," Cypriana says tensely. The action has begun. Now it should unfold according to the detailed plan devised by Bardou and the committee. "Most people up here are ill."

"Is it a contagious disease?" Lefrèvre asks with forced casualness. Ground has anticipated that such a case might occur. Space might contain deadly bacteria. If they attacked the SP, they could also spread to the International Space City. That would spell disaster, not only for the ISC but possibly for the earth.

Lefrèvre feels hot and cold at the same time, as the possibilities flash across his mind. The SP has to be quarantined immediately!

"Contagious?" the woman on the screen repeats. "We don't know anything about it yet. But so far nobody up here has died from it." She turns her fine profile as if looking at somebody else.

"Who is presently in charge?" Lefrèvre asks, debating with himself if he should make decisions without checking with Mancini. By ten o'clock the epidemic might have spread uncontrollably.

"Pierre Bardou. Or do you want to talk to Dr. Behrmann, our physician?"

As though Bardou were making up Lefrèvre's mind, his face appears behind Cypriana's.

"The situation is unclear," Bardou says, his words tumbling out as though driven by barely suppressed panic. "Within half an hour about forty people collapsed. Some have developed a high fever. Could you send up some serum?"

"What kind of serum?"

"I'll let Dr. Behrmann describe the symptoms to you. I'm sure the Pasteur Institute in Paris has all tropical diseases computerized. You can check with them."

To Lefrèvre's surprise Behrmann's round face appears beside Bardou's, as if he too has been waiting in the background. Lefrèvre feels an apprehension: was this scene staged for his benefit?

"Chest pains, rapid pulse, sore throats, but lowered body temperatures," Behrmann says. "I've never seen anything like it and cannot classify it. Mrs. Stern is trying to analyze the bacterial strain which shows up in the feces. The closest I can guess is that this is a variation of the common cold, except that it attacks rapidly, almost paralyzing the body. It is accompanied by severe nerve pain."

"Send up a large astrocommuter, in case we have to evacuate some of the patients," Bardou adds.

"You know that isn't possible without the unanimous consent of Ground," Lefrèvre says sharply, his suspicions growing. This epidemic might be a ploy to get some of the prisoners back to earth. "You certainly are aware of the rule."

"I understand." Behrmann's gaze shifts unhappily on the screen. "We'll have to wait for the serum to be sent up. By then we might have determined the bacteriological strain."

"Ask Jules Dubois to come up," Bardou suggests. "Though you might have to quarantine him afterward."

"Why Dubois?"

"I have a good relationship with him. And we need somebody from Ground who would help us."

"I'll see what I can do," Lefrèvre says vaguely. Thoughts are racing through his mind. If Ground decides to let the epidemic run its course, the people up there might die. But then a permanent grave would circle the earth.

The screen becomes dark.

Lefrèvre sits down and forces himself to think calmly. The Pasteur Institute has to be alerted immediately. To send up Dubois would not be a bad idea; Dubois pretends to be the prisoners' friend. He is a double agent, catering to the inmates while reporting to his superiors. Of course he will have to be decontaminated on his return and quarantined for awhile. An astrocommuter should be sent as soon as possible. Lefrèvre decides to act right away and to inform Mancini later; the older man will appreciate his resourcefulness.

Lefrèvre feels that his promotion is assured. Unknowingly he is following Bardou's and Behrmann's scheme.

# XIV

Landings and departures at the Space Prison are guided from the central control room. They are semimanually directed by Jan Van Buren, the Dutch engineer (life sentence for having led a fascist uprising in Rotterdam in which twenty-three people lost their lives). Van Buren watches the approach of Astrocommuter 232, with Jules Dubois on board, streaking from the Paris spaceport toward the SP. The space ferry turns in a graceful curve, flying parallel to the SP, overtaking it, turning around to face the port, slowly merging with it at almost zero velocity. A slight shudder runs through the SP at the moment of contact, an almost imperceptible tremor like that of a door closing in a house. Van Buren has guided the astrocommuter to a perfect landing.

He feels the pounding of his heart as if it were a motor in need of a tune-up.

The inmates have been informed of the spacejacking plan. Vera Stern and ten prisoners decide to stay behind. But they also want to cooperate in the venture. They too put their lives at stake. Of the ten, four are terminal cases, wracked by cancer, two suffer from Parkinson's disease, one has Hodgkin's tremors. They are the lost patrol, expendables, but as important to the inmates as a group of kamikazes. Should the escape not succeed or should Ground, after a deal with the escapees, go back on its agreement, they will blow up the SP.

His life sentence has not changed Van Buren's personality. In his dreams he visualizes the ISC exploding in a hundred thousand parts, arms, legs and torsos flying through space on a journey to the infinite. For Van Buren the ultimate thrill of life is death.

Miranda watches him. He is acquainted with Van Buren's warped mentality.

"No violence," Miranda says in a flat voice. "Understand, Jan, no violence. Those are the committee's orders. If you resort to violence, you'll be killed. By me!"

"Why should I become violent?" Van Buren grins at him, his emotionless eyes glittering like cut glass. "We haven't rendocked the ISC yet. Who knows what's going to happen?"

"After we've boarded the ISC, no violence!" Miranda repeats with an uneasy authority. Miranda, Latin by background and temperament, hates everything Nordic—that world without sun, the world of war, conquest and brutality. Van Buren seems to personify all that.

"The two thirty-two just docked," Van Buren announces, pointing at the television screen that shows the inside of the hangar.

The nose of the ferry opens. Dubois emerges, carrying two suitcases. Bardou walks up to meet him, and their voices come over the loudspeaker.

"You're a brave man, Dubois," Bardou says, relieving him of one of the suitcases. "You're taking chances."

"I don't think so." Dubois's lean, craggy face breaks into a smile. "We have a club down there: the friends of the SP. I'm the president!"

"Bastard," Van Buren whispers as though Dubois could hear him. "Double-crossing bastard! Pretending to help us!"

The sound of the ISC's celestial music emerges from the loudspeaker, growing in strength, then fading slowly.

"In two hundred and twenty minutes I'm having a drink at the ISC's bar," Van Buren announces, combing his long blond hair with his fingers. "I'm looking forward to a Genever over ice!"

On the monitor he watches Dubois walk with Bardou down the corridor toward Ibbotson's office; they bob and float like marionettes. Cypriana trails them, wearing a miniskirt and high boots on her long, elegant legs. She swaggers prettily, as if modeling clothes. Behrmann, beside her, kicks himself off the floor and descends softly.

"We at Ground are prepared for any epidemic in the SP." Dubois watches the empty corridor. "Everybody's ill, I take it?"

"About eighty percent of them," Behrmann says. "It seems to be a mutation of the common cold. We don't have enough antibiotics to treat everyone."

Dubois swings his small suitcase. "I have them here. Enough for a big hospital!"

They reach Ibbotson's brightly lit office and enter.

"Where is Stig Ibbotson?" Dubois asks, looking at the empty desk.

"You can't meet him," Bardou says. "I'm replacing him for the time being."

"He's sick too," Dubois concludes. "Well, no urgency." He walks over to the videophone as if he were at home on the SP and presses a series of buttons; Lefrèvre's face appears, drawn and tired from lack of sleep.

"Just to report that we arrived safely," Dubois announces jauntily. "The situation is well under control!"

"Glad it's nothing serious." Lefrèvre manages to produce a tone of sympathy. "Now I can take a rest. Call me at home if you need me."

"I don't think I'll need you." Dubois waits until the monitor screen becomes blank, then flicks off his switch. He folds his hands on the table to steady himself. "Have you seen the latest reports on weightlessness? They've found that the human body suffers after all, producing sleeplessness, nervousness and circulatory difficulties. Have you had that experience?"

"Not yet," Bardou says. "Of course, I avoid the zero-gravity section as much as possible. Why don't you join us for dinner, Dubois? Try our delicious algae omelet!"

"No thanks," Dubois says. "I just came to deliver the antibiotics. I'd better return now."

He looks toward the door where Hallstadt and Van Buren enter. Dubois smiles, amused by their swinging bodies, dancers in slow motion. They bounce up and down, coming toward him with a sliding rush. More people enter. Dubois finds himself surrounded by people.

"I'd like to see Stig, even if he is sick." Dubois twists out of his chair, but Van Buren and Hallstadt push him back. Dubois suppresses a sudden terror.

"You'd have to talk to bones," Hallstadt says, his eyes all pupil, resting on Dubois intently.

"Bones!" Dubois gasps. "Why bones?"

"He's dead."

"When did he die?"

"A couple of hours ago. We dragged him to the air lock. You know—the air lock? Close the door, open the outside door. The vacuum does the rest. Very quickly, painlessly."

"You killed him?" Dubois searches for Bardou's face but finds it cold and hard.

"It was necessary," Guzmán says unemotionally. "We have our laws. He broke one, the most important one. Now we want you to call your pilot, Dubois!"

"What for? I'm just leaving." Dubois feels himself trapped, confined in a box which closes its walls around him, becoming smaller and smaller, suffocating him. He breathes in gasps.

"Do what we tell you. Call the pilot," Van Buren says with an ease which carries a deadly threat. Again Dubois tries to get up, but the hands behind him slap him down forcibly.

"You're going to get yourself into trouble," Dubois manages to say.

"Hardly," Van Buren whispers behind his back.

"Call the pilot," Bardou repeats.

"And if I refuse?"

"We wouldn't stand for that," Hallstadt says flatly. "We have nothing to lose. What can possibly happen to people who are buried alive?"

"I'm your friend." Dubois anxiously searches the eyes of the people surrounding him.

"Are you? Prove it," says Bardou.

"What's on your mind?" Dubois' racing thoughts crowd each other trying to analyze the situation. "Are you going to keep me and the pilot hostage for concessions? That wouldn't make sense in the long run. Tell me what you want."

"Call the pilot," Hallstadt repeats almost soundlessly.

"All right." Terrified, Dubois pushes himself up. His feet leave the floor for a moment.

"You can talk to him on the videophone. We connected our communication system with the ferry's. Go ahead. You won't get hurt," Hallstadt says.

"Hurt?" Dubois echoes, and a sudden fury grips him. "If I don't return within three hours, you'll be in trouble! If anything happens to me or the pilot, the SP's supplies will be cut off by Ground and you'll slowly die."

"We know that," Bardou says, his lips forming an indulgent smile. "That's just the threat we want to get rid of."

"You can't force Ground to do anything, damn it!" Dubois flares up. "Don't you have any sense left?"

"If you don't cooperate, you'll end up in the air lock," Behrmann says calmly.

Shaking, Dubois switches on the videophone. The pilot's face appears.

"We want you in here, Orsatti." Dubois forces himself to speak calmly and casually.

"What about that epidemic? I don't want to expose myself," the pilot objects.

"No danger, none whatsoever. We need you for advice."

"What's all this?" the pilot says uneasily. "What kind of advice?"

"This is an order," Dubois says as sternly as he can manage. Before the pilot can answer, Van Buren switches off the videophone.

Dubois sits quietly as if in a drugged immobility. The prisoners are silent, but the air seems charged with menace.

"Couldn't I get some kind of explanation from you?" he finally asks.

"You will soon." Bardou's eyes are grave. "We need your assistance. I don't want to be melodramatic, but I don't think you're paid to die for Ground."

Dubois shakes his head jerkily. "There isn't that kind of money around. But how do you expect this to work? You can't succeed, whatever it is you're planning." Dubois tries to form his expression into his familiar one of friendliness and understanding. He smiles. "All right—I'm with you, even if I don't agree with you. But there's no escape, if that's what you have in mind. You're defeated before you start. You're dealing yourself a bad hand."

He slides the cliché in like a hypodermic needle.

None of the prisoners answers him.

# XV

The International Space City's casino is built in the style of London's nineteenth-century Crystal Palace, with clinging lianas winding around Victorian pillars that reach for the globe's high ceiling. It was the architect's whim to contrast an earthman's fanciful designs with the sparse expanse of the galaxy which displays its stars and planets behind the casino's transparent walls.

The constant rotation of the ISC changes the view from night to day, from star-studded panels to that of the clouded earth below.

The continuous low murmur of the gambling casino sounds like the lapping of waves on a distant shore. Conversation seems to consist of monosyllables. Croupiers' monotonous voices rise above the muted din. The ivory balls rolling around the roulette wheels, the dull click of dice hitting the felt walls of the crap tables, the well-oiled hammering of slot machines accentuate the acoustics of the gambling casino. The players crowd the tables or glide soundlessly over thick carpeting.

Lee is floating in limbo, waiting for his letter of resignation to be acknowledged by Ground.

Wandering anonymously through the casino, Lee Powers enjoys being a nonperson. He is awaiting acknowledgment from Ground of his resignation; he hopes they won't refuse to accept it. If they insist that he fulfill his contract, he will fight to break it. Lee is determined to leave the ISC.

"I've heard the news and can't believe it," a voice says behind him. The spell of detachment is broken. Kenneth Andrews, his black face grinning with friendly mockery, holds out a small tower of chips. "You always were a gambler. Try your luck with these!"

"I never got pleasure gambling for money," Lee says, vaguely amused by Kenny's condescending manner; he knows that beneath it lies a real concern for him. "When I win, it doesn't mean much to me, and when I lose, I regret the money lost."

"You're losing both ways," Kenny replies, looking levelly at him. "Whether they accept your resignation or decide to reject it."

"I forgot you've been monitoring every room. You listened to my conversation with Jerry Tomlinson." Lee takes the chips from Kenny.

"It's my job to know everything," the young head of Security says solemnly. "That's what you expect from me, isn't it?"

Kenny puts a small pile of gambling chips on a square of the roulette table. As the croupier sings out "*Les jeux sont faits*," he watches the ball roll counterclockwise and fall into a slot. The wheel comes to a stop.

"*Douze*." The croupier pushes a high stack of chips toward Kenny.

Kenny looks boldly at Lee, his eyes daring.

"Why don't you take a crack at it?"

"I don't want to tempt fate. I want fate to move without my interference; that's my way of diminishing risks. But you go on; run your luck."

"Do you think I have a streak coming on?" Kenny puts all his chips on number eight, but then cautiously distributes some on other squares. "If so, I'd like you to stay with me. Okay?"

The ball falls into a slot. The wheel stops. The croupier pulls in Kenny's chips, except for one which he fourfolds. Kenny picks up the remaining chips.

"I just broke even."

"That should be my answer to you," Lee says. "I have to make a change, Kenny. One day you'll have to make decisions that will change the direction of your life, too. You'll have to make it alone; nobody can advise you. And if you ask somebody's opinion, you'll only be asking him to agree with what you've already decided for yourself."

"If that's the case, I should get your job. I couldn't work for anybody but you—or be boss myself," Kenny says boldly.

Lee laughs. "I have only one vote in the council. You know the trouble I had getting you your present position. Don't run too fast, you might fall flat on your face!"

"I haven't so far. I took a lot of business off your shoulders. You don't even have to talk to Judge Nicopulos about the Czech incident; I squared that case with him. The judge agreed with me."

"That was an obvious decision. No government has legal rights up here. The Czechs must've known that; they just tried to bully their way through."

"Now they're playing against their elusive prisoner, hoping he'll lose his money." Kenny nods toward a small table. "*Vingt-et-un, Pontoon*—Svoboda plays against the 'punters.' They're out to break him. If he runs out of money he won't be able to stay up here; he'll have to go back to earth. Smart, those detectives!"

"Is he winning?"

"It's chance against skill. If the game were based on skill, I wouldn't bet on the two detectives. Svoboda has brains; I checked on him. He's a member of the Czech underground. He absconded with the party's money and came up here. That money would have been impounded by the Czech government. But it isn't our business to play police."

Svoboda is holding the bank. He deals one card face down to each player. They make their bets, putting piles of chips in the middle of the table. Svoboda looks at his card, carefully lifting one corner.

"Double the bet," he mutters in a toneless voice

which nevertheless betrays his hatred for his opponents.

"Where did those detectives get all that money?" Lee asks, watching the duel.

"They cashed government checks. I'm sure they were ordered to bring Svoboda back by any means. They know he's a compulsive gambler. Svoboda turned up in the casino five minutes after Judge Nicopulos released him. He didn't even book a hotel room."

Lee watches Svoboda lose. The detectives' pile of chips mounts. They grin smugly, which seems to taunt the thin man. His mouth pressed into a tight line, Svoboda takes a handful of chips from his suitcase.

"He's stupid. Does he want to commit suicide?"

"That's what I suspect," Kenny answers, his eyes on Svoboda's shaking hands.

"The ISC's become a hideout for criminals and drones," Lee grunts angrily, scanning the faces around the gambling tables. A group of beauty queens clusters around the roulette wheel. The faces of rich old men and women, hypnotically concentrated on the dice, the cards, the round ivory balls are frozen in expressions of abstract bliss. They have chosen the Space Hotel as their permanent home, having left earth for the excitement of a world that offers them every amenity of life in a small space. In previous years, Lee remembers, these people traveled endlessly in luxury liners. One of them paid four hundred dollars a day for a suite cruising on the same ship for twenty years until he discovered the Space Hotel. Lee watches a long-legged cocktail waitress dressed in the red uniform of the ISC pushing coins into a slot machine—tips she has received and quickly gambles away. A fine madness permeates the air, an invisible low ceiling of greed and depression.

"Whom do you include in your list of criminals?"

Kenny asks. "The big corporations that keep their headquarters in Globe Eight to avoid paying taxes in their own countries? Before they moved to the ISC it used to be Liechtenstein. Now it's the ISC."

"You're paid to run security, not to express your social conscience," Lee growls at his young friend, to cover his feeling of guilt. The luxurious decadence of the Space Hotel wouldn't have happened without his initiative and ingenuity in devising the satellite. "I suggested many times taxing those corporations heavily, but the board of directors overruled me—they're part of the game too, directors of the big corporations or stockholders. But why worry so much about money? I never cared much about it. If I'd put all of my efforts into making money, I might have become a millionaire. So what? The ultimate aphrodisiac is power, not money. Money and power aren't synonymous—you can have power without a bank account."

"You don't usually talk so abstractly," Kenny said. "I think it must be the demon of being unfulfilled that's speaking in you."

"You heard that from Tomlinson," Lee says, his anger evaporating suddenly.

"True. But you accuse me of running too fast and also remind me that power is the ultimate pleasure in life. I'm not a dreamer like you; I have my feet on the ground. Have you?"

"You can't have your feet on the ground when you're dealing with space." Lee walks slowly through the crowd, repulsed by the casino's tense atmosphere, the oppressive murmuring unhappiness around him. "All I ever created is mechanical. Mankind hasn't changed on account of the City in the Sky or the flights to other planets. So far I've only devised hardware. I don't know if I still control the machines or if they control me. That's what I want to explore. If I find the answer, I'll know what to do."

"What about me?" Kenny steps in front of Lee.

"I've done all I can for you; from now on you'll have to go your own way. Drop that father image of me. Don't try to emulate me. Didn't you just say you had your feet on the ground? Don't hold onto a man who's floating."

"I never thought you had human frailties," Kenny says, a worried look etching his face. "That's where I got most of my strength, from watching you."

"Tomlinson said I should try to discover my soul!" There is laughter in Lee's voice, a mixture of sarcasm and real amusement. He turns soberly to Kenny. "I want you to alert all department heads, all of them —Rubikov, Bergstrom, Nicopulos, Robaire, Alende, the heads of the laboratories and communications. Tell them to be ready at any time to meet me at the Holographic Room. I'm expecting a call from Ground; I want them to be present."

"You never used to do that," Kenny says uncomfortably. "You always made your own decisions."

"If Ground accepts my resignation, they'll have to name my successor. I certainly won't suggest one."

"What about me?" Kenny asks. "You told me you'd support me."

"I won't support anybody, damn it. I want to get rid of my responsibilities. If I suggest you and you give them trouble, I'm back where I came from. I want to be free."

"Even of me?"

"I want to sever every tie, every relation to the ISC. And you're part of it."

Lee suddenly realizes he is fighting an unfocused impatience—as if his fate were waiting for him somewhere and he must find where to meet it soon.

# XVI

Globe 8 resembles a city street with building fronts, shops in their ground floor, glittering windows displaying treasures of the earth below: Winston of New York, Cartier, Tiffany, Van Cleef and Arpels, Barone of Milano with its multicolored necklaces, diamonds glittering like suns from other galaxies, reflecting the quartz lights hidden above the showcases.

In the back rooms of the globe, giant world corporations have their headquarters: Royal Dutch, Leverholm, Bofors, Dupont, Van den Bergh, the steel works of Schneider Creuzot, Krupp, Bethlehem, Indian Rubber, the Union des Banques Suisses—in a short stroll of two hundred and fifty feet, a hundred-billion-dollar financial capital is concentrated. These corporations control the commerce of the world. They pay taxes to the City in the Sky, one-quarter of one percent of the gross receipts. Within three years they paid half the building costs of the ISC. The ISC itself is big business, blue-chip shares, a favorite investment of the affluent.

Lee strolls down the globe's street. Its gravity one makes him feel heavy, like walking on earth. He likes the diminished gravity in the ISC's axis, where he can take giant steps, float for ten feet, barely touching the ground to reach his small apartment. His two rooms are almost bare, furnished with a table, two chairs, a spartan bed, a narrow closet holding a few clothes. Lee does not want possessions; they chain him to an earth which he likes to leave, to float in space without ties except those which fascinate his mind and inspire his imagination.

He stops in front of a jeweler's window. A few people stroll past him, their voices painfully loud in his ears.

Lee looks at the sparkling stones in the show window, gleaming eyes staring back at him sightlessly, confined in an emotionless beauty, useless and pampered. The diamonds and gold surround stones of gray and reddish colors; they are rocks from the moon, some from Jupiter and Venus, brought back to earth by unmanned spacecraft. Diamonds are less fashionable among the superrich than the dull rocks from faraway planets.

A male hand appears in the window, carefully picking up a tray with moon rocks. Lee dimly makes out a man and a woman, the salesman and a customer. The woman is slim, her movements graceful. Suddenly she turns, as if Lee's gaze has called her.

Lee steps back in surprise. A subconscious thought emerges, a feeling that he has come to Globe 8 specifically to meet her. The woman appears in the doorway of the store. Lee looks into eyes as light as those of a bird of prey. He sees a flash of recognition in them and realizes she is looking at him with resentment.

This is the woman he saw at the Paris spaceport of Le Bourget. What was her name? Susanne—Susanne Lesuer?

"I expected to run into you up here," she says, her low voice betraying rage and indignation. "You bounced me off that space ferry and made me waste a day of my life. How can you be so callous about other people's time? I expected to find you in the bar with a girl with some name like Fifi or Kiki. Or what else are you doing up here?"

"It wasn't my choice," Lee answers. "I certainly didn't pick you to be taken off the astrocommuter."

Suddenly Lee feels an elation for which he can find no reason. "But let me apologize in the name of the International Space City," he adds quickly.

Her eyes change color, become darker.

"That girl at the ticket office told me who you are. That was her apology. Now you apologize for *her*!" A wry smile crosses the woman's face. "She said she was forced to put you on the astrocommuter because you have priority even over the heads of governments." She smiles again, more warmly this time, and her face with its translucent skin and fine bones becomes animated and full of mirth. "A man as important as you should have his own space ferry and not steal seats from common travelers like me who are in a hurry."

Lee points at the colorless stones in the window. "To buy moon rocks?" He joins her mood, happy that she has set her anger aside.

"I couldn't afford even the smallest one. I only wanted to touch them. Three billion years old! That's like touching eternity. If I had the money I'd like to wear one; it would make me feel less earthbound."

"I don't like to feel earthbound either." Lee reaches out his hand and touches her arm, an impulsive movement prompted by an overwhelming desire to contact her bodily. She does not seem to resent his touch, but he quickly withdraws his hand.

"I believe I owe you more than an apology," he says, feeling the shell of his isolation crumbling. "I'm going to make amends. I'll give you a rock brought back from Mercury."

She looks at him wide-eyed and steps closer to him. Though she appears to be tall, she reaches only to his shoulder.

"Why should you do that?" she asks. "Mercury! That'd be worth at least a hundred thousand dollars. How could I accept a gift like that?"

But there is a strong excitement evident in her mouth and her parted lips.

"It has no value for me. I'm not a geologist. Its only value for me is that it might please you."

"Do you have it in your pocket?" She holds out her hand; narrow and long-fingered, it seems to embody a peculiar cruelty, like a small vicious animal asleep.

"I'll have to get it from my room."

"Ah! And you want me to come with you to pick it up!"

"We could go to a bar and you could wait there while I fetch the rock. Or you might like to come with me."

"We could do both," she decides. A glow of gaiety and abandon emanates from her. Lee cannot guess her age. Is she twenty or thirty? She vacillates between child and woman.

The bar is crowded. The mob pushes Susanne close to Lee. He is aware of her breasts, her hips, her face close to his.

Every one of the two thousand guests of the ISC seems to have taken refuge in this bar. The barmen fill glasses in a frenzy. A huge mirror along one wall doubles the number of the people. More are continually rushing in.

Lee watches himself and Susanne in the mirror. She holds onto him to avoid being swept away by the tidal wave of bodies. The low room echoes with shouts and laughter, calls for drinks in a dozen languages.

"What's the matter with them?" Her mouth is so close to his that he feels the warmth of her breath. He puts his arms protectively around her, holding the people away from her. "Are they closing up and everybody wants a last drink?"

"No. The ISC soon will pass through a cloud of concentrated neutrinos. That happens every day at this hour."

Her eyes open wide, questioningly.

"M. Robaire will tell you," Lee says. "My explanation might be too technical."

A man seemingly in his late twenties stands beside Lee. But Susanne discovers a careful makeup around his eyes and cheeks; closer scrutiny reveals his age is closer to fifty than to thirty.

Lee introduces them: "M. Marcel Robaire, world-famous manager of the hotel. Susanne Lesuer."

"You remember my name!"

"How could he ever forget?" Robaire says with a graceful movement of his hand. "But let me rescue you, mademoiselle. This crowd is mad, mad, mad!"

He lifts both his hands over his head and snaps his fingers. At once two waiters appear and clear a path through the noisy crowd.

"Addicts!" Robaire's young-old face breaks into a slow smile, careful not to disturb the smoothness of his makeup. "As for the cloud of neutrinos, I can only give you a scientific explanation, though not as precise as Dr. Powers could provide."

They reach a door and enter Robaire's office. It is a small room with a couch covered with soft material of deep red, a carpet of red velvet on the floor. Two low, heavily upholstered chairs stand beside a Louis XV writing desk.

Robaire closes the door, shutting out the noise from the bar.

"Insanity every day at four P.M." He sighs and waits for his guests to sit down in the plush easy chairs before he slowly lowers his trim body to the seat behind his desk. "I'm afraid you'll have to wait a few minutes until the panic is over."

He looks at Susanne with admiration and a concentration which seems to eliminate Lee from the room. Rolling his chair close to her, he leans toward her but discovers an expression in her eyes which makes him retreat again. He leans back in his chair, sighing.

"Neutrinos are elementary particles having a zero mass and charge. Zero mass, that's what the scientists call it. For us laymen, anything with a zero mass doesn't exist. But for them, it does. The neutrinos are in a radioactive decaying process. They pass through the ISC or the earth or anything else as if it didn't exist. And they do mysterious things to drinks up here."

"Mysterious?" Susanne looks at Lee for clarification. Robaire at once moves closer to her to get her attention.

"Yes, mysterious! The neutrinos interact with the hydrogen molecules in the alcohol and make the drinks very peculiar."

"Peculiar?"

"Yes. People who take a drink while we move through the neutrino cloud feel as elated as if they just had made love. Love when it is good is very good. When it is bad, it is still good!" Robaire laughs. "Really, I have a drink at the right time and have a very gratifying reaction," he says without taking his eyes off Susanne. He seems hypnotized by her presence. "Sorry we've passed that cloud already. It takes only a few minutes, or I'd have offered you a Campari dolce with lemon. Sweetness in the drink seems to enhance its effect."

Susanne looks disbelievingly at Robaire, then says mischievously, "Now I understand! That's why Dr. Powers took me to the bar! Very sneaky! But I certainly will remember the hour when not to see you, M. Robaire."

She gets up as though terminating an interview. Robaire quickly rises.

"I understand. You're for the real thing. So am I," he says smoothly.

"I don't need a substitute aphrodisiac," Susanne says, and touches Lee's sleeve lightly. The gesture has an intimacy that isolates Robaire.

"Any time you wish, please call on me," Robaire says. He suddenly looks his age. "I'll do anything to make your stay at the ISC pleasant."

"I have to be in London in a few hours." She holds

onto Lee's arm. "Thanks for the information—it's a good warning." She smiles coolly.

The crowd in the bar has thinned out when they leave Robaire's office.

"Your friend is creepy," Susanne says. "He tries very hard, but I don't think he likes girls."

"Do you call men who don't like girls creepy?" Lee asks, amused by her reaction. "Robaire is a genius when it comes to running a hotel."

"Is he married?"

"His wife is very intelligent. She runs the Space Hotel's newspaper, a kind of gossip sheet. They have two children. That'd disprove your theory."

She shakes her head. "That doesn't prove anything. I know that type; my partner is like him. The gentleman doth protest too much!" She smiles at him suddenly. "*You* certainly don't!"

"Still interested?" Lee asks, feeling her nearness vanish as she slides her arm out of his.

"In what? The Mercury rock? Of course."

Lee opens a door with a passkey. They find themselves in the spoke which connects the axis with Globe 8. As they walk, Susanne observes with astonishment that their steps become longer, her body lighter.

"That's dizzy!" she exclaims. "Is that diminishing gravity?"

"Yes. It will get more pronounced."

"It's like dancing!"

She takes a giant step, jumping high, and touches the ceiling of the spoke.

"All my life—since I was three—I've practiced to remain weightless in midair, just for a fraction of a second! To be suspended! To escape my earthbound body! But here . . . here . . . it's—" Again she jumps and, opening her arms wide, descends gracefully like a floating autumn leaf.

"You're a dancer?" Lee asks.

"I'm with the Royal London Ballet."

She poses in midair, her fine head and long neck bent backward, sensually exposing her throat, and still floating, she unfastens her hair to let it cascade down her back.

"Unbelievable! I'll never leave this place!" she cries, her black hair swirling around her like a dense cloud.

Lee wants to catch her in his arms, but she is deeply engrossed in her dance. He watches, fascinated, as she pirouettes in midair, a feather in the breeze yet retaining her own will and choice of direction.

He recalls the moment when he saw Susanne for the first time at t[illegible]e Bourget spaceport in Paris. Was that the turn[illegible] point that Tomlinson told him would appe[illegible]ife? "Unaware to the consciousness, the human mind slowly prepares itself for a complete change and acceptance of ideas, emotional or otherwise," Tomlinson said. "A catalyst will trigger in you a whole new approach to thoughts and feelings."

Lee opens the door to his apartment, sensing it as the portal to a new future.

"Is this where you live?" Susanne lands softly at his side and enters the room before him. "Not cluttered at all—it's like your mind," she says with appreciation. Suddenly she drops the skirt she has been wearing and kicks off her shoes; they fly through the air and hit the opposite wall with a clatter.

She stands in front of Lee in black leotards which cover her body completely, clinging to her slim figure, outlining in precise detail her straight shoulders, small breasts, well-proportioned arms with hands not much wider than her wrists, long, graceful legs that seem to flow from an almost hipless pelvis. Her ivory face with the oversized light eyes looks at him with a knowing smile, conscious of her attractiveness.

He takes her in his arms without resistance, weightless, alive, warm. As he kisses her, they leave the floor, suspended, a kiss in space. He is aware only of her body, not of the ground below. Their kiss is a dance; every small movement turns their torsos lightly in air.

Slowly they descend in a tight embrace. He looks into her eyes, finds softness and warmth there.

Lee pushes himself up still holding her. He feels the slim curve, the elegant backbone in his hands, like a fine instrument that could produce music.

"I promised you a stone," he says to those incredible light eyes.

"Just let me touch one." She holds out both hands like a child.

Lee half floats over to the chest of drawers which protrudes from the wall. In a wooden box lie a handful of small rocks.

"They're all from Mercury. Take as many as you like, take them all."

He holds out the box. With tapered fingers she chooses one stone.

She lifts it to her eyes and stares closely at it for a long moment; then suddenly she throws the rock to the ceiling. As the stone slowly descends, she leaps, catching it in midair.

The rock from Mercury becomes her partner in an air dance. She plays with it, catlike, lets it rise and descend slowly, drifting from wall to wall. She is Giselle, Odette, Princess Aurora, Clara playing with the nutcracker toy, Coppelia the doll—the repertoire of the Ballet Royal woven into one seductive dance for her audience, one man, Lee. He watches her eyes flash as she passes him, holding out one hand as though she were desperately trying to join him but were taken away by an immutable fate. Her movements enchantingly change into magic.

Susanne catches the Mercury rock with both hands. Her face is close to Lee's, but upside down, and as her mouth touches his, she turns in air and lands silently on point. As he puts his arms around her, oblivious of time and place, the silence is suddenly broken.

A sound no louder than the striking of a match comes from his shirt pocket, an electronic alarm. Susanne, pressed close to him, feels the instrument's vibration at her breast.

At once she retreats from his embrace.

"What's that?" she asks, her eyes wary.

"An emergency call," Lee says.

"Do you have to answer?"

"They call me only when it's very important. Yes. I must answer."

He awakens, leaving a world which has just opened its gate to him. With one long step he reaches the wall behind the desk.

"Don't," Susanne says, fear in her eyes. "Don't answer!"

"It'll only take a minute."

A panel set invisibly into the wall lights up as Lee activates the videophone. Kenny's anxious face appears in the screen.

"I got a Siglar," he says hurriedly his eyes scanning Lee's room, discovering Susanne. "An astrocommuter is in trouble. The pilot asks for an emergency landing."

"Contact all spacecraft. Tell them to stay away from the rendock globe until the emergency is over. Have the crash crew stand by. I'll be over in a minute."

"All right. I'll send out alarm one."

The picture becomes dark; the videophone reintegrates with the wall.

"You seem upset," Susanne says, her face anxious but still retaining a hint of the ethereal quality she embodied a few moments ago.

"Those emergencies sometimes turn out to be troublesome. If the ferry's guiding system fails, it might crash inside the landing globe."

He takes her tense face between both of his hands.

"I must go to the monitor room."

"To leave me now—*c'est une peine forte et dure*," she says almost inaudibly and steps back to look at Lee.

Her image engraves itself on his soul, a picture too beautiful to be forgotten.

"Don't be long," she says. "I'll wait for you here."

# XVII

"The ferry isn't in any immediate danger as long as it doesn't land," Kenny says. "I've put the conversation between Imoto and the pilot on tape. Let me run it for you." Imoto is the engineer in charge of guidance system that directs astrocommuters to the hangar.

"When did he hear from the ferry for the first time?" Lee asks. He tries to shake off the fey image of a beautiful female gracefully floating as in a dance underwater, her body so vibrant to his touch.

"We're holding the ferry on radar and are in voice contact," Kenny says as he switches on the voice tape.

"Mayday! Mayday!" The words are charged with anxiety. "This is Ferry two thirty-two. Do you read me?"

"You're in contact," Imoto's soothing voice answers. "Come in, Ferry two thirty-two."

"We've lost our inertial platform and manual backup. Require guidance aid. Immediate! Immediate!"

"Ferry two thirty-two. We have you on radar. Steady as you go. In nine minutes you'll be three thousand feet off our port bow. Hangar deck at thirty degrees."

Lee switches off the tape. "Get me direct connection with two thirty-two," he says to Gay Chan. On the monitor screen of the console above him the dark void of space appears, and in the distance the tiny shape of the distressed ferry.

"Who's on board?" Lee questions the ferry.

"Pilot and passenger from Ground," the ferry answers. The pilot's voice is muffled as though he were talking through a piece of cloth.

"Destination?"

"Ground."
"Point of departure?"
There is a pause, and the voice is almost inaudible, riddled by static. Finally the pilot says, "SP."
Lee turns to Chan. "Get me Ground immediately."
"We will need velocity control for possible rendezvous," the ferry's pilot says.
"Explain how your path came so close to the ISC trajectory. Procedure forbids your trajectory," Lee broadcasts. A quiet warning bell is sounding in the back of his mind.
"Original path was nowhere near you. Guidance failure during propulsion mode. Utterly no control during propulsion. Glad to be safe and near you. Thanks for aid."
"Stand by, two thirty-two," Imoto says. "We're checking control."
"We need. . . ." The pilot's voice dissolves again into static.
"Reading you," Imoto says. "Differential velocity eighty-seven feet per second. Turn one hundred eighty degrees and then apply velocity. Switch to manual control. We will be well in your sight. Maneuver will bring you to sixteen hundred feet off our port. Acknowledge."
"Understand." There is a breathlessness in the pilot's voice which increases Lee's alarm. He has the impression that different voices speak at different times.
"They'll be safe for seven minutes," Imoto says to Lee. "I'll need your consent to let them land."
"Hold them." Lee turns to the screen above his head where Lefrèvre's sleep-lined face appears.
"You called me, Powers?"
"Yes. Ferry two thirty-two is in distress. What do you know about her?"
"She just left the SP," Lefrèvre says, his face visibly

shaking off drowsiness. "She shouldn't be in your vicinity!"

"Check on her, right away," Lee says.

Lefrèvre's face fades from the screen as he hurries away.

"Did two thirty-two tell you she's coming from the SP?" Lee asks Imoto.

"She's in trouble. No time to ask," Imoto replies.

Lefrèvre's face again forms on the screen.

"There's the pilot and Dubois on board," he reports. "If prisoners were on it, they'd register on our board—they carry transmitting devices in their bodies which they can't discard. All devices are still on the SP."

"If this conversation goes on much longer, two thirty-two is going to crash into us." Imoto's voice too has an edge of anxiety. "She's not steady."

"Repeat: Failure at propulsion mode," the ferry's pilot says urgently.

"Stand by," Imoto repeats tensely.

"Does Ground confirm propulsion mode?" Lee asks.

"Confirmed by Ground," Imoto replies. "I checked with them earlier."

"We would like to come aboard for repairs." The voice from the ferry has become strong, as if it were in the control room with them.

"Lefrèvre, two thirty-two wants to dock on the ISC," Lee says to the face on his screen. "I'd prefer her to land on earth."

"We can't handle her—we have no voice contact," Lefrèvre says. "Can you dock her?"

"I can guide her in," Imoto confirms.

"Docking ISC confirmed by Ground," Lefrèvre says, obviously happy to get rid of a responsibility.

"Landing okayed by Ground," Imoto repeats.

"What's your opinion?" Lee asks Kenny, unable to free himself from an uncertainty.

"Ground checked the two thirty-two. Imoto can dock her," Kenny says. "What's your objection?"

"Two thirty-two, follow instructions. We will direct you into hangar, using laser guidance. Use an MX6A visor for protection for yourself and passenger. Laser will be directed from hangar door. Before you move, pick up laser in your manual guidance optic. Use optic visor too."

"Read you loud and clear," a muffled voice says from the ferry.

"No motion until directed. Confirm," Imoto says.

"Your franc. Say when."

"Advise your passenger away from windows until hangar entry."

"Advised."

"Laser now five degrees off your bow below pilot window. Low-power density. Should be highly visible."

"Hangar very clear in view."

"Perform manual search for optic."

"Is the crash crew standing by?" Lee asks. He feels a strange sense of unreality, as though hearing his own voice from a speaker grille.

"Crew standing by," Indru confirms.

"Locked on manual optics," the pilot's voice says. "Rendezvous laser seems to be working."

"Seems to be?" The tenor of Imoto's voice becomes anxious. "What do you mean by *seems*—does it, or not?"

"Right for now, right for now!" the pilot answers quickly, as if afraid the ISC will stop him from landing.

"Approach at two, repeat two feet per second until laser intensity falls off, then drop your delta V to zero point five feet per second. We'll signal by voice also when laser intensity drops."

"My radar measures one thousand forty feet to hangar."

"Proceed," Imoto orders.

"Three hundred forty feet from hangar."
"Null your velocity, null it."
"What happened to laser intensity?" the pilot's muffled voice comes over the speaker.
"Null your velocity, damn it!" Imoto's voice loses its calm composure. "Do you want to crash into us?"
"We're at zero delta V per instructions and standing by, make it two hundred seventy feet."
"Good. So do we," Imoto answers, relieved. "Stand by. Hangar door will open presently. On my instructions proceed to zero point two feet per second. Proceed until ferry's nose is just inside; then null your velocity again. Careful. Proceed."
On the screen which depicts the hangar from outside television cameras, Lee watches the hangar's door open like the shutter of a camera. The ferry slowly drifts inside. Like dragonflies, other astrocommuters and astrotugs dot the space, waiting for their turn to dock.
"Moving at zero point two feet per second," the pilot reports.
"Null velocity now."
"Done."
"Now stand by. We have magnetic robot probes which will attach to your ship and bring it to a docked position. Lock out your propulsion system. Make all systems benign."
"All systems benign," the pilot reports.
The hangar's shutters close like those of a camera.
"Stand by. Hangar repressurization in three minutes. You will open your door when hangar and your inside pressure equalize. Watch your pressure gauges."
Five minutes later Kenji Imoto, guidance operator of the International Space City, will be dead, his skull exploded by a rocket bullet.

# XVIII

Lying prone on the floor of astrocommuter 232, Bardou's body echoes the tremors of the landing gear, which, grabbing the ferry, guides it to its docking position. Cypriana is close beside him, her breath sounding harsh and fearful in the tense silence. A mass of bodies, coiled like tightly wound springs, fill the ferry and its cargo space: fifty-two people, motionless and inert to escape the detection of the ISC's radar devices.

Orsatti, the pilot, sits numbly in his seat, Hallstadt at his side, pressing the muzzle of a homemade rocket gun against his kidney. Miranda lies on the floor, holding a microphone covered with a cloth to disguise his voice. His teeth are bared like those of an animal at bay. Dubois, his mouth taped shut, his hands roped behind his back, leans against the ferry's wall. Though he promised the committee to cooperate, they don't trust him. His eyes express his fierce anger.

In kaleidoscopic images the last moments of the ferry's departure flash through Bardou's mind: Vera Stern, silently watching the men enter the astrocommuter. A few faces swimming in the back of the SP's deserted corridor, inmates too old or too feeble to join the venture.

Hallstadt has trained the spacejackers as if for a commando raid. The layout of Globe 5 of the ISC, minutely drawn like a military map, is marked with strategic information. Hallstadt relied mostly on the memory of inmates who had been on the ISC, but also on the SP's own construction, the original pattern of the City in the Sky. The attack has been rehearsed to its last detail dozens of times. Every one of the attackers has his objective assigned to him. The goal is to reach the duplicate control room of the atomic reactors and to seal off Globe 5 from the rest of the ISC. The limited number of men can occupy only a small part of the International Space City.

Hallstadt does not anticipate any resistance. In his opinion the operation should take no more than five minutes to complete, which will leave the opposing force no time to organize.

Bardou is assigned by the committee to conduct negotiations with the ISC's officials. In case of his death, Guzmán and then Kentu will take over. The succession of command has been worked out to the last member.

The ferry's vibrations stop. From his low viewpoint Bardou observes the ceiling of the hangar with its crane, catwalks and giant vents to pump in or suck out the hangar's air. He watches the ventilators whirl, feels the ferry being buffeted by artificial wind. Then the blades feather and come to a stop.

"Hangar pressure equalized with your inside pressure." Imoto's voice comes from the ferry's speaker. "Glad we docked you safely. Open your door."

The ferry's door slides back. As though propelled by an explosive force, Hallstadt jumps out, followed by Van Buren and the most agile of the group of desperate men.

Bardou quickly gets to his feet. A glass cage inside the hangar contains the switchboard which controls the flow of air, the radar monitor system and the hangar's machinery. Bardou stares at the faces of Imoto and his two assistants, petrified in shock. The door leading to the globe glides back, revealing the crash crew, dressed in fireproof suits, carrying emergency equipment. They too are frozen in terror.

"Shut the doors! Pump out the air!" Kenny's voice screams from Imoto's loudspeaker. Propelled into action, Imoto turns to reach for the compressor switch.

With two giant steps Van Buren reaches the glass booth and fires a rocket into Imoto's face. It disappears in a spray of blood, which in the almost zero gravity splashes in all directions. Bardou reacts to the shot as if he too were hit. Suddenly the attack has taken on the aspect of a murderous crime; he has become the leader of a group of killers.

Hallstadt's strategic plan unfolds as rehearsed. In less than two minutes the attackers pour out of the ferry.

Imoto's blood floats through the hangar, thousands of tiny rust-red globules climbing slowly to the ceiling to be swallowed up by the air filtration system.

Bardou finds himself face to face with the crash crew, clumsy-looking in their asbestos suits, carrying fire-fighting equipment and stretchers.

"Don't move," Bardou shouts. "Nobody will get hurt. Don't move!"

He races down the tube which leads inside Globe 5. A horde of men tear ahead of him. They pour into adjoining rooms and into the center control station with its electronic gauges, levers and switches that govern the flow of the ISC's atomic power.

The attackers quickly back four stunned ISC operators into a corner. Miranda leaps toward the giant switchboard and pulls the levers that lock the emergency doors, isolating Globe 5 from the rest of the ISC.

Except for the heavy breathing of the men and the muffled sound of their steps, the attack is carried out in silence. Only now Bardou becomes aware that his body is drenched in cold sweat; it pours over his face, burning his eyes. He wipes them with the back of his hand.

"We're lucky!" Miranda's voice is shrill and wild. "They have only one reactor in operation. The two others are shut down. We've got them by the throat!"

"Van Buren shot a man!" Bardou says hoarsely.

"What else could he have done?" Miranda exposes his teeth in a savage grin. "Half a minute later and we would've suffocated. All of us."

Bardou stares unbelievingly around the control room. Never in his life has he been exposed to violence. Now he was forced to cope with it, as if it were part of his life.

"You'd better stop that Gandhi streak in you and face the facts," Miranda says fiercely.

Bardou takes a firm grip on the panic inside him and walks over to the cornered men in white overalls.

"Nobody's going to harm you," Bardou says. "Just cooperate, and you'll be all right!"

"What's this all about?" one of the men asks. His face has a puffed, sickly look. "Who are you?"

"Never mind who we are," Bardou says, and abruptly realizes that a desperate gloating is welling up within him at the sight of these frightened prisoners. His plan is going to work!

"I want to know," the man insists desperately. "What is all this? Are you trying to spacejack the ISC?"

"Spacejack?" Bardou repeats sarcastically. "I thought I coined that word."

# XIX

"You are requested to stay in your rooms or wait at the restaurant for further information." The voice blares from every loudspeaker. "This is the ISC's management speaking. Stay in your rooms. Don't walk around. Stay in your rooms. An announcement will be broadcast soon."

The lobby is crowded with a mob of pushing, excited people, a tightly packed mass floating like molasses in cold water.

The calm, impersonal voice from the loudspeaker seems to have no influence on the crowd. They mob the reception desk, where a dozen pale, nervous clerks use the same words to answer identical questions.

"Why did they stop the ferry to Sydney? I have to be in Sydney tonight!" a woman shouts. "You can't shut me up here!"

"We'll have an official announcement soon, madam," the harassed clerk says.

"You can't keep me up here!" a burly man with a large head barks at a female clerk, his gross face close to hers. "I'm going to sue this hotel for all it's got, damn it! I'll lose a million pounds if I'm not in London today!"

"The official announcement will be delivered within the hour," the girl says mechanically, a sensation of helplessness rising in her. She wants to shout out her fears just as these people do.

"The announcement will be broadcast to every room and to the restaurants, but not to the lobby," one of the clerks says, inventing a lie to get rid of the people who bother him. "I can't tell you more at this time, sir, madam!"

"Let's go to our room," a tall woman says to her

husband. "Those people behind the desk can't tell us anything."

"I'm still going to sue them," the man answers gruffly. "You had to travel via the Space City. Next time I'll take a train! It's faster!"

The clerks pick up the ruse which one of them invented. "The message will be broadcast to rooms. Please return to your rooms."

The crowd is slowly thinning out of the lobby.

"You know if the ISC blows up, we'll all become satellites, our bodies flying through space forever," one of the clerks says to the girl in the red uniform beside him.

"Satellite François!" she says with a forced smile. "You'll be registered by every observatory as a satellite that twinkles only at female stars. The roving eye satellite!"

"In ten thousand years they'll fish us out of space and put us in a museum. *Homo sapiens*, twenty-first century! And they'll have their theories about us as we have about cavemen," Francois says. He looks around. "This *is* a cave. A cave in space! We're the cave people. But if anything ever happens to this contraption, wow!"

"Then why did you take this job?" the girl in red asks.

"If I knew I'd tell you," François says, aware of the girl's longing for assurance. "I can only guess that we have some technical upset in Globe Five that makes it impossible to send off ferries. That's the only explanation for this mess."

"Mess?" the girl repeats; the word seems wrong to her, inadequate. She senses greater dangers.

"We'll know when they finally come out with an announcement. That is, if they decide to tell us the truth. So far everything here seems to be working all right. No change in gravity." He exercises a small hop like a novice ballet dancer. "The air is breathable. Everything's normal, except that they had to shut down Globe Five."

"What's in that globe that can go wrong?"

"I wouldn't know." François puts his arm around her and feels the slight swelling of the edge of her breast. "But if something should happen, I'd rather be in my room, with company and a bottle of champagne." He moves his hand slowly, stroking the side of her breast, and the girl moves closer as if to encourage him.

"I feel lost," she says softly.

"Let's wait for the announcement in my room, shall we?"

"We're on duty."

"I don't think anybody will miss us for the next hour or two," François says. He's had his eye on this girl for the last week. She is young, with a rounded body and the wheat-blond hair of the Dutch. François has a girlfriend, a Spanish woman who works as a cocktail waitress at the gambling room. His affair with her is punctuated by violent quarrels that end in embraces and heightened sexual feelings. Would the fear of impending death also sharpen the emotions of sexual intercourse?

"When the emergency's over, we can be back in no time," he says.

"All right," the girl says, her fears overpowering her. She wants to find sanctuary in François' arms, even for a few short minutes.

A voice comes from the loudspeakers.

"This is your captain, Lee Powers, speaking." His voice travels through the rooms of every globe. "The management apologizes to the guests of the International Space City. We have an emergency in the hangar for arrival and departure of the astrocommuters. Until this emergency has been relieved, we ask your indulgence for the delay in your departure. There is no danger for anyone. The restaurants will serve free food, and there will also be entertainment in the ballroom. Please bear with us. We'll keep you informed of our progress."

The voice stops, and music replaces it.

"He didn't tell us anything," François says. "Shall we withdraw to my princely suite?"

"I don't think I want to anymore," the girl says, taking an impatient step backward to get out of François' reach. "I'm going to wait here until the emergency is over."

She resents François' jocular attitude, aware that he is making light of his own fears and trying to use her as an escape from them.

"Don't get into a funk!" François says. "When your number is called, you go, not before!"

"I know," the girl says. "But what do you do if it's a wrong number?"

# XX

"Those bastards won't get out alive!" Kenny Andrews hisses through clenched teeth, his dark, knife-scarred face vicious in its frustration. "They started with murder, and they'll end up dead themselves!"

Twenty-five television monitors in the control room are trained on the interior of Globe 5. Six monitors are connected with Ground, with Mancini in Geneva, Lefrèvre in Brussels, McClore in New York, Vassilev in Moscow, with the Sydney Ground station, with the Tokyo spaceport.

The room is crowded with executives and supervisors of the ISC, among them Judge Nicopulos. The old man has a cynical smile on his lined face, as if he were enjoying the situation. He sits quietly in a corner, observing the commotion around him.

"I don't want any sound or picture from here transmitted to Globe Five," Lee orders Gay Chan, who is operating a switchboard.

"I've pulled the main switch of Globe Five's communication system. Nothing can get through," Chan reports, again probing the dials on the control board.

"Bastards!" Kenny repeats. Confronted with the first major crime on the Space City, he finds himself impotent to meet the emergency. He wants to jump through one of the monitor screens onto the spacejackers. "They won't leave the ISC on their feet. They'll float out into space!"

"The computers should have been programmed for such an attack." McClore's elongated face, grim and angry, stares accusingly at Lee from the New York monitor screen.

"Well, they weren't," Lee says. He feels detached from the near hysteria around him.

"You can get out of a computer only what you feed into it," Tomlinson says, addressing all monitors. He too seems unperturbed, his stability increasing in proportion to any mounting pressure.

"We had to ground the ferries all over the world," McClore complains worriedly. "We'll have to send out some explanation to the press before they start to speculate."

"Tell them we have technical difficulties in the hangar; that'll hold them for a few hours. In the meantime I'll try to negotiate with these people. It's obvious what they'll demand from Ground."

Lee focuses the zoom lens on a group in the hangar, until one face covers the monitor's screen. That face shows fear and abject determination, like a cornered animal that can only fight or die.

"Anybody know this man?" Lee asks.

"That's L'Ardonnier," Lefrèvre says. "He broadcast revolutionary speeches for the rebels when they occupied the Congo mines. He was sentenced by my country to life imprisonment. Yes, it's L'Ardonnier—he was insane, and he still is!"

The screen shows a group of agitated people. Imoto's twisted body lies on the floor. Nobody bothers to hide his smashed face which, grotesquely disarranged; looks like a carnival mask. Some globules of his blood are still floating about lazily. One of the spacejackers steps unconcernedly over the corpse, waving a rocket gun. The lens depicts, in a wider angle, a group which seems to be confused and uncertain what to do next.

"How did they escape undetected from the SP?" Mancini in Geneva growls. "They're supposed to carry implanted tracing devices. Didn't those show their movements up on your monitors, Lefrèvre?"

"Those devices still register on the SP," Lefrèvre says, confused. "They show all these prisoners still back on the SP."

"How could that be possible?" Mancini asks, pushing back a white shock of hair. "Somebody explain that to me!"

"That question is of secondary importance at this moment," Vassilev cuts in coldly, speaking from the Moscow screen. "We must solve this situation before it gets completely out of hand."

"Somebody must be in charge of those bandits," Mancini barks. "Find him, Powers. Make a deal with him! Any deal! This outrage must be stopped immediately and at any cost!"

"We know what they want," Lee says. "They want their freedom—what else is there for them to demand?"

"Obviously," Hawakawa seconds on the Tokyo screen. "Let's consent to anything they ask. We don't need to keep our word. What can they do once we have them back on earth?"

Lee watches the monitor's eye switch from the huge hangar with its spacejacked ferry to the living quarters of Globe 5, its kitchen, the storerooms crowded with faces unfamiliar to him. He starts to count them. How many are there? Forty? Fifty? His camera scans the storeroom. The spacejackers gorge themselves with food they obviously have not tasted in a long time: breaking raw eggs in their mouth, greedily tearing chunks of ham with their teeth, ladling canned fruit from containers.

"Just send them to New York," McClore says, and chortles. "I'll deal with them. But don't give in too quickly, Powers, don't make them suspicious!"

"They suffered an unusual and barbaric punishment," Lee says. "If I were a prisoner on the SP, I'd be among those men!"

The zoom lens of his monitor stops on Bardou's lean, intelligent face. He stands near the atomic control panel. A tall Asian girl is with him. Talking with graceful movements of her long, slim hands, she seems to be on intimate terms with the man beside her. Another man approaches them, built like a wrestler, his head incongruously refined-looking on the gross body.

"You approve of these bandits' actions?" Mancini says, shocked. "Then you're the wrong man to conduct the negotiations!"

"I'm still in command of the ISC," Lee says grimly. "Those people have genuine grievances. I'm going to listen to them and help them if possible."

"I know how to get rid of those bastards without getting into conversation," Kenny says with a cold fury. "Let me go outside the ISC. I'll shoot a few holes into Globe Five and the vacuum will take care of them in no time."

"And if they open any door, that'll take care of the ISC too," Lee adds, shaking his head. "No violence as long as I am in command!"

"You've sent your resignation," Mancini reminds Lee. "We accept it. We need a man like Andrews to deal with those outlaws."

"Ground consents to my resignation? Good!" Lee grins at the faces on the monitors. "But I want your acceptance in writing. Send it up with the next ferry!"

Calmly he shuts off the monitors which connect the ISC with Ground, except for one, Lefrèvre's.

"Who is that man on Monitor Fifteen?" Lee points at Bardou.

"Pierre Bardou, a French professor of economics. He published secret papers which embarrassed the French high command," Lefrèvre explains reluctantly, uncomfortable that he has been singled out by Lee for questioning.

"Sentenced to prison for life!" Lee grunts disgustedly. "Who's the man beside him?"

"Jules Dubois. I dispatched him to the SP with provisions. He's supposedly working for us. I can't understand. . . ." Lefrèvre has a sudden suspicion that his trusted man switched sides and is helping the spacejackers.

"And the girl?"

"Cypriana Maglaya, convicted of murder."

"Political, no doubt," Lee snorts. "They send only political prisoners to that space Siberia." He checks himself with a short laugh. "Maybe I *am* the wrong man to conduct the negotiations! Get the board of directors together, Lefrèvre. I'm going to arrange a holographic conference between Ground and those people. I don't think Ground would ever accept my decisions. Let them talk to those people themselves!"

"I still don't know why we should go through all that trouble," Lefrèvre mutters. "Why waste time making a deal that Ground will never honor? Andrews suggested getting rid of them painlessly—painless for them and painless for us. I'm in favor of that!"

"I didn't ask what you're in favor of," Lee says with cool authority. He switches the Brussels monitor off. Lefrèvre's twisted, guilt-ridden face disappears from the screen before he can object.

"We should never have had to face this situation," Kenny grumbles, smarting under his limited authority.

"The tyranny of the 'should,' " Judge Nicopulos says from the back of the control room. His sunken features lift in a sardonic smile.

"Turn on the sound and projection to Globe Five," Lee orders Ferranti and Chan. "Project my picture on the monitor in the atomic control room. I want to talk to Bardou."

# XXI

"I'm going to decide about when and if, nobody else," Bardou says with determined calm. "Any unilateral action won't be tolerated. Hallstadt will see to that."

"And Jan," Hallstadt answers softly. "Whatever you say, Bardou. You're the boss." He carries two rocket guns around his neck, his hands casually close to them.

"That video eye is watching us," Miranda says, pointing at the lens on the wall.

"There's one in every room. Why not smash them?" Shepilov suggests. "Constant surveillance, I've lived through that most of my life!"

"I want them to watch what we're doing," Bardou says. "I don't mind if they overhear what we're saying." With a labored smile he takes a cup of coffee from Cypriana. She looks militant in a safari outfit, a rocket gun at her slim waist, her hair severely pulled back. An Amazon, as ruthless as Van Buren or Hallstadt, Bardou surmises. He watches some of the spacejackers drift aimlessly by, their minds floating in euphoria now that they are in control of the ISC. They are not the same meek downcast people Bardou knew at the Space Prison. They talk agitatedly, their eyes shiny, and their movements have the quick jerkiness of eager impatience.

"It takes two thousand years to make a Christian and two minutes to change him back into a heathen!" Bardou mutters to no one in particular. Dubois overhears him and steps close to him. He carries a plate with food. Behrmann has set him free, even removed the tape from his mouth with care not to inflict any pain.

"I heard you," Dubois says. "Now all those people have an objective. Freedom, life—if they die fighting for it, that won't make much difference to them. Dying too can have its elation. It's an objective! Without it, life doesn't exist."

"Sorry you were treated roughly. There was no choice," Bardou apologizes to Dubois. "No time for amenities!"

"It was bad form, though," Dubois says with a grin. His eyes find the video lens. "They must be confused about me." Hungrily he lifts food to his mouth. "Doubly confused since they see us talking like friends. They don't know if I'm working for them or for you. I don't even know myself!"

His voice carries an apology to the video lens.

"They haven't contacted us yet," Kentu says anxiously. "Why don't we get in touch with them?"

"No rush," Bardou says languidly. "Time is on our side. It weighs more in our favor with every hour we wait. They're in a hurry; we're not." But the picture of the dead man stays with him, painfully burned in his memory.

"Nothing ever goes according to plan," Hallstadt says, sensing Bardou's distress. "Better prepare yourself for more of the same, boss. Death is a constant companion from the moment we're born. I said 'thank you' to the dead man in the hangar. That corpse serves a purpose. The ISC knows we aren't bluffing!"

The video screen in the atomic duplicate control room lights up. Lee's face appears on it, behind him a shadowy crowd of slowly moving bodies. Lee's eyes wander around the control room, checking it expertly, and settle on Bardou.

"Pierre Bardou." His voice is matter-of-fact, without urgency.

"That's my name." Bardou turns without haste, matching Lee's calm.

"My name is Lee Powers. I'm in charge of the ISC."

"I know."

"I want to thank you for keeping the ISC's reactor going; everything's working well, no trouble so far." Lee is trying to establish a rapport with the tense, intelligent face on his screen.

"Thank your crew, not me. Nothing is going to change as long as they cooperate. Everything is under control up to a moment. . . ."

"What moment?"

"Your choice, Powers—if you make one more mistake, I can't guarantee what my people might do. *L'animal est très méchant, quand l'on attaque il se défend!*"

"Yes, the animal is very mean, it dares to defend itself when it is attacked. But who attacked whom?" Lee matches Bardou's sardonic smile.

"One of your men attacked us, by giving an order to open the hangar doors. The vacuum of space would have suffocated all of us. We had no choice. But a man died who could still be alive."

"I don't want to argue that point," Lee says. "Let's come to an understanding. There are three thousand people on the ISC, among them women and children. They are cut off from the earth."

"So were we for years," Bardou answers.

"You're holding part of the crew prisoner!"

"All of us are prisoners. I'm yours, and you're ours. Your men wouldn't be any better off in your part of the ISC, and here they serve a purpose."

"Come over to my office," Lee suggests. "I'm sure we'll find a solution to our mutual problems—and without interference from outside. I'm top man at the ISC."

"Don't," Hallstadt warns Bardou. "As soon as we unlock one door, they'll rush us. They have the weapons."

"If they do, Miranda is going to pull out the reactor rods. The reactor will melt, and the ISC will freeze up before they can evacuate it," Bardou says, looking at Lee.

"You don't need to threaten us," Lee says, suppressing a sudden anger. "I'm aware of how you could wreck the ISC; I could suggest a few more ways to you, in fact. But you didn't take over the control panels just to threaten the people up here. You want to find a solution to your own problem."

"Justice—that's all we want." Bardou is sharply aware of the power he wields, a sensation alien to his life before now. "We demand justice. Whatever crimes we committed, they've certainly been matched by the cruelty of our sentence. We don't feel guilty. But how can we protect ourselves from being double-crossed by Ground?"

"I don't know," Lee says hesitantly. "They'll have to prove their sincerity. But we'll find a solution. I've called a meeting of the board of directors, and I'm sure the departments of justice of the concerned countries will also send representatives. I won't take part in it. I want to be an arbitrator, neutral."

"Don't believe him!" Miranda hisses, his eyes hard, locking away his fury. "He's like a dog that wags his tail and bites you when you come close."

Bardou disregards Miranda's outburst. "How do you suggest conducting the meeting? By videophone?"

"By holographic transmission. There's a room in Globe Five equipped for this. Holograms and laser beams. My men know how to handle the equipment. You'll meet people from Ground but as three-dimensional projections. Your image will appear on earth, among the people of Ground. I'll be sitting in on both negotiations. You don't need to open the door for anybody, Bardou. But I want the discussion to start as soon as possible. So far we've kept the news of this from the world press and from the people up here. We can't afford a panic."

"A panic would help us immensely, Powers!" Bardou says with a hard smile. He is surprised by his callousness—is cruelty a basic emotion in every living being? "Don't rush us, Powers. My friends are in no hurry. They haven't had so much space to move about for a long time. This is quite an improvement on their former way of life."

# XXII

For Marcel Robaire, manager of the Space Hotel, the frantic exuberance in the giant ballroom has the taint of a dance of death. The sandstone relief of the "dance macabre" in his hometown Basel in Switzerland is engraved in his memory: Death leads the procession of the king, the queen, the rich, the poor, beggars, cripples, men, women and children, even babies. The baby speaks to Death: "Oh, Death, I do not understand, you want me to dance and I can't even walk!"

The restaurants and the ballroom are crowded as though it were New Year's Eve. A band from Uganda is playing a catchy new rhythm, the "Long Banana." Dancers move in unconscious imitation of African sexual rites. In an adjoining room England's famous stand-up comic, Franky Pettycomb, delivers puns about the closing of Globe 5.

The videophones are in constant contact with the earth; business goes on hectically between the tycoons marooned on the ISC and their enterprises. The quotations on international stock exchanges show a marked decline of the ISC shares.

Marcel Robaire's office is crowded with young men and women, "futs" as they call themselves, dressed in colorful attire. They look handsome in narrow-cut dresses of batik material, created in the latest fashion center in Nairobi, East Africa.

Robaire collects handsome people the way a philatelist collects stamps. Their presence charges his life with youthful excitement. The light in his luxurious office is dimmed to a mysterious crepuscular glow which softens his features and makes him look years younger. It also hides his perfect makeup.

"Ah, m'dames, m'sieurs!" His capped teeth glisten luminously. "When will we ever have again such a fortuitous chance to relax without being tortured by guilt? Enjoy, enjoy! What was yesterday's news? What will tomorrow bring? That is if there is a tomorrow! There might be one for you but not for me. *Qui sait*? I welcome this happenstance which commands us to relax. When the hangar reopens and the ferries again arrive and depart like moths in summer, this enchantment will be over! Ah, I've learned that most people are busy only to escape from themselves. Their excitement has to be created by outside stimulations. How many of us have inner resources? That's why this kind of emergency is a present to all of us. Duties evaporate; appointments are canceled; obligations cannot be enforced; responsibilities lose their meaning. One is confronted with a *force majeure*, just because a hydraulic lift in the hangar does not work properly. How amusing! Enjoy—enjoy! Spend these hours of abandon recklessly. They are stricken from the pages of the book of conscience. Let's be gay—as long as the champagne holds out."

He talks incessantly to keep his terror caged. Silence would break its prison. The ISC is under siege. Kenny has told him about the spacejacking and the imminent danger to the satellite.

Robaire's small hands move with charm, describing tiny circles, casually touching one or the other of his enchanted guests who sip their free champagne from fine cut-glass goblets. Two of his favorite young waiters, slim, graceful, keep the glasses filled from Magnum Veuve Cliquot bottles.

In the back of Robaire's mind lurk thoughts of his family. André, who studies in Oxford and visits the ISC only on weekends. Claudine, in Lausanne at a girls' finishing school. Valerie, his wife, is in Rome to arrange color printings for the ISC magazine which she edits. They will be safe. But will he ever see them again? A premonition of disaster fills his being. Robaire is not a forceful man. For years he went to a psychoanalyst to find out why he could not stand up under mental pressure. The analyst finally suggested to him that he should never have married, that he was sexually more inclined toward males than toward females. Having become a family man put a severe crimp in his personality, which disturbed his adjustment to the world around him.

Robaire is a gifted administrator, and in space he is his own boss, independent, detached from his former existence. Frantically trying to break with hidden desires he is unable to face, he surrounds himself with girls picked for their beauty, a beauty that in itself makes them unreal and untouchable for him.

"Tonight will be the ball of the year!" he announces. "A celebration second to none!"

An exquisite young man's face bends close to him. Large green eyes smile at him in abandon, a Mona Lisa smile, an offering he knows he cannot accept. He always keeps himself at a distance from such a temptation, knowing that the carefully constructed walls of his inhibitions would crumble.

A tall man enters his office; his head reaches the upper door frame. He supports himself on a cane. His small dark eyes are alive with a restless excitement, his face pale but for a bulbous veined reddish nose. To Robaire's consternation he is dressed in a flowery robe which hides the white wraparound of the hospital patient. At once Robaire jumps up from his chair and opens his arms wide, waving the small crowd out of his office.

"Shush! Shush! I have a very important guest! Shush, please leave, dear people. Gaston and Erin will serve you champagne in the ballroom. Excuse me, excuse me!"

His dazzling smile freezes into a mask as he closes the door behind his visitors.

"Mr. President!" he says, lowering his voice. He reverts back to the able administrator, businesslike, efficient. "What can I do for you?"

James McVeigh slowly settles into one of the soft easy chairs.

He mutters, his breathing hard and labored, "I was trying to find Lee Powers. But I ran out of steam. This place is so damn big that I couldn't find my way around, so I landed at your place, Robaire. I wish I hadn't—the way the gravity is here I feel like I weigh a ton!"

"You could locate Dr. Powers on the videophone," Robaire suggests, looking genial and unconcerned as though making small conversation, trying to hide his shock at McVeigh's physical deterioration.

"I sneaked out of my prison. Bergstrom wants me to die there, but I won't cooperate. I have a method of postponing death, Robaire! Using the videophone would have told Bergstrom's secret service where I was, and they'd have dragged me back to the hospital. Give me a glass of water!"

He produces a small vial and swallows a couple of pills to stimulate his heart. Robaire pours water from a crystal carafe.

"The ISC is in trouble," McVeigh continues calmly. "Well, that condition has to be dealt with. I had many near disasters in my life when I was in the White House. You know about that attack on the hangar, don't you? Powers would have told you."

"Andrews did," Robaire answers, calmed by the presence of this man who still exudes a great power. "He's the head of security."

"It's the damnedest thing, that spacejacking! I wonder how it can be solved. Ground won't give in to those criminals; they'd lose face. They'd rather see the whole damned Space City fly apart, I'm sure of that. Easy for them to decide when they're down there!" McVeigh puts a nitroglycerin pill under his tongue. "Get Powers for me, Robaire. But don't tell Bergstrom where I am; he's liable to drag me back to my bed. That bed! It's like a coffin to me. I know as long as I'm on my feet I can run away from death. But being confined in that hospital, what can anybody think about except being sick? Every little pain becomes a threat. Damn those doctors! They put ideas in their patients' heads! If you think of death, he's liable to pay you a visit. A visit? One single visit, that's it! He mostly comes by invitation." The pill takes effect, and McVeigh breathes regularly. "Now get Powers for me on the video."

Robaire obligingly presses buttons on the videophone console. The operator's face appears instantly on the screen.

"Find Dr. Powers for me. It's urgent," he says. He switches off the transmitter and turns back to his guest.

"Whatever I can do for you," he says with a sweeping gesture of his white, small hands. He smiles amicably, hiding his wish to get rid of McVeigh as soon as possible. Should McVeigh have an attack in his office, the embarrassment to the hotel would be headlines.

To his relief Powers' tense face appears on the screen. He looks down at McVeigh.

"You called me, Mr. President?"

"I want to offer you my help," McVeigh says. "I understand you're in the shithouse, my boy." He smiles thinly, enjoying Robaire's shocked reaction. "You can't even call in the marines. What are you going to do about this mess?"

"I've asked Ground to negotiate with those people,"

Lee says calmly. "So far the spacejackers haven't done anything drastic. There was an unfortunate shooting during the attack, but that violence is over."

"I want to help you negotiate with them," says McVeigh. "I'm damned good at it—did it for years with all kinds of people, heads of state, unions, industry, the Congress. I believe I know how to settle disputes."

"Your prestige would be invaluable," Lee says evasively. "But your present state of health . . ." Lee is afraid McVeigh might transform a crisis into a permanent disaster. He is a gambler, a man who prides himself on his brinkmanship.

"Worry about your own health!" McVeigh says angrily. "When I have my new heart, I might push your wheelchair, Powers. People who look as healthy as you sometimes drop dead quickest. We hypochondriacs take care of ourselves. You don't; you take health for granted. So don't give me any crap about my condition!" His face is flushed. "You have my offer; take it or leave it. But you'd be foolish if you didn't avail yourself of a professional like me. You don't know how to negotiate. Or do you?"

"I'm sure Ground will be very happy to have you conduct the negotiations with those men," Lee says distantly, freeing himself from any responsibility concerning McVeigh. "You're known as a man on whose word one can rely. And those people from the Space Prison know it."

McVeigh's long face folds into an ironic mask. "I wouldn't say that, Powers. There's always that credibility gap between promise and fulfillment. Politics is built on it. Did you tell the passengers about the spacejacking? Or did you invent a plausible explanation? Ground told the press some story about a technical failure in Globe Five. But that bubble might burst at any moment, Powers. You can only lie so long, and when the truth catches up, you'll have a first-class panic on your hands."

"I hope by then we'll have made a deal with those people," Lee says. He feels exhausted; he wants to be alone with himself to organize his thoughts, to charge himself with new energies. "I hope we can start negotiations in one or two hours, or as soon as I get clearance from Ground. The conference will be conducted by holograph, since the SP people don't want to let us enter Globe Five. Up to that time I don't think the prisoners will do anything rash to endanger the ISC. Of course they have that possibility, since they control the atomic panels."

"Why have negotiations at all?" McVeigh asks impatiently. "You haven't any options. You have to accept their demands."

"I know, but they'll ask for guarantees. That's where I see the difficulties. How can we guarantee our word to them?"

"Let me think about that," McVeigh says, putting another nitroglycerin tablet under his tongue. "Why did you call on Ground for those negotiations? They'll mess up everything, as usual."

"I can't speak for the board of directors," Lee says. "My only hope is that they'll be reasonable since the ISC is a three-hundred-billion-dollar international investment. They might decide to sacrifice people on principle, but not money!"

"Yes, yes, even the Communist countries are capitalistically inclined when it concerns their purse!" McVeigh laughs dryly. "If I were in charge of making a deal, I'd do something drastic, novel, extreme!"

"What do you suggest?"

"Being honest. Keep the promise. Speak the truth. Stick to our commitment. Convince them that we really mean what we say. If honesty ever becomes the norm and not the exception, the world would finally have peace."

"You tell that to Ground!" Lee answers with a look of appreciation. "But can we convince them? I hope you can, or the exploded parts of the ISC will circle the earth for the next five hundred years!"

# XXIII

In the large conference room of Globe 14 Evgeny Rubikov, chief engineer of the ISC, and Gerald Tomlinson, assistant to Lee Powers, supervise the installation of the holograph projector for the impending conference with the spacejackers. In Ground's conference room in Geneva an identical device is being set up.

Tomlinson, his body accustomed to the reduced gravity in the hospital section, breathes laboriously in the greater gravity of Globe 14. His lined face shows the strain of his damaged heart.

Thirty chairs stand around the wide elliptic green felt table. This is the room for international conferences, impersonal, without decor in order not to give preference to any national culture.

Three technicians in ocher work clothes connect cables to the man-high laser transmitter and the holograph projectors.

"Testing, testing," Rubikov says in a low voice. Hidden microphones carry the sound to Ground in Geneva and to Globe 5. He manipulates dials on a small console in front of him.

At once a ghostly shape materializes in the room: another table is superimposed over that in the conference room, a mirage overlapping the real table like images in the viewfinder of a camera.

"Adjusting," Rubikov repeats. His face looks pained, reflecting the same worried expression etched into Tomlinson's features.

Apparitions move in the room: technicians in similar clothes as those worn by the men in the conference room. They are stationed on earth, in Geneva in a similar room containing an identical table.

"Adjusting," a bodiless voice replies. The image of the second table fuses with that of the first one.

"Calling Globe Five," Rubikov broadcasts. "Five. Are you ready, Five?"

"Adjusting," a voice answers from Globe 5. "Adjusting."

The image of a third table becomes discernible, smaller than that in Globe 14, and the technicians in the occupied globe mistily take on a three-dimensional substance, slowly becoming distinct.

"Adjustment complete," the technician on Ground says without emphasis. "See you clearly. Can you see us?"

"Image clear," the man in Globe 5 answers. He walks forward toward Rubikov, an ethereal body generated by the laser beam's lithium niobate crystals.

"Images clear in Globe Five," Rubikov acknowledges.

"Cut off the sounds," a voice behind Tomlinson orders quietly. Tomlinson turns to find Kenny standing there, his lean, dark face an angry mask.

"What for?" Rubikov asks, irritated. "We aren't quite synchronous yet."

"Leave the images on, just shut off the sound," Kenny demands. Alarmed by the urgency in Kenny's voice, Rubikov complies.

"I don't want those spacejackers in Globe Five listening in," Kenny mutters. "I'd like to know why Lee wants to go through all this mess. Conferences! Negotiations! You can't make deals with those people. There's a better way. . . ."

"Is there?" Tomlinson asks, his voice inhibited by his labored breathing.

Kenny says, "I should have objected at the beginning to Lee's demand for a holograph conference. I've placed all my security guards around Globe Five. I could get rid of those criminals in minutes! They wouldn't have a chance of wrecking anything." Despite his efforts to keep his voice down, Kenny is speaking loudly.

"What do you suggest?" Tomlinson asks patiently. Often he has been the arbitrator between Lee and this impetuous young man.

"Globe Five has holes like a Swiss cheese—ventilator shafts, electric conduits big enough for people to crawl through, passages for repairing cables, pipes that those bastards don't know exist. Floor plates can be unbolted. I'm going to stage a general assault on those murderers. At D-hour my men will suddenly pop out all over the hangar in Globe Five and blow those space-jackers to bits. Lee made a rule: no automatic weapons on the ISC, just handguns and clubs." He laughs sharply, his face grim. "I stored machine guns, rapid-fire rifles, ray guns, a whole arsenal! I didn't tell anybody, not even Ground. Now we're going to find good use for all that stuff!"

"Have you told Lee about your plans?" Tomlinson asks quietly.

"Lee is a pacifist. I'll bet when I get rid of those bastards, he'll fire me for acting against his orders. He's against any kind of violence. What does he think is happening here? They started the violence by killing Imoto."

"One drawback, Kenny," Tomlinson says. He feels weak; the excitement of the last hours has left him with a sensation of unreality. He hears Kenny's voice as if it were coming from a faraway room. Gathering his strength, he gets up from his chair, leaning heavily on his cane. "If you miss a couple of those men, if you can't kill all of them in one fell swoop, they could still sabotage the ISC. And what about the crew in Globe Five? They'd be in danger."

"I've thought of that, too. We'll try not to hurt them. But we have to weigh the fate of those twenty-two men against the three thousand on the ISC. Wouldn't you rather lose twenty-two people than three thousand? I've learned one thing in life: Fight violence with violence. There's no other way to stay alive."

"So you want my consent. Why?"

"You're the second-in-command; you'd take over if anything happened to Lee. Something has happened to him. He gave up his leadership and turned the negotiations over to Ground."

Rubikov speaks up. "This is war, Tomlinson. Andrews is right. If those people don't get what they want, they're prepared to die. And they'll make sure that we join them."

Tomlinson watches Rubikov warily.

"Shouldn't we try peaceful means before we start shooting?"

"Nothing will come of the negotiations. Nothing, damn it!" Kenny explodes. "Don't be a fool, Tomlinson. If you give them time, they'll become more and more suspicious. They now believe we want to make a deal with them. They're off guard. That's the time to strike!"

"The decision has been made, Kenny." Tomlinson takes a step toward the door. "No violence. That's an order!"

"Globe Five has been occupied for almost three hours. How long do you think we can hide the situation before we have a full-sized riot on our hands?"

Kenny's eyes dart around the room where ghostly images from Ground and Globe 5 move noiselessly about, three-dimensional specters without substance.

Two phantoms enter the conference room in Globe 5, Bardou and Miranda. Bardou is rigid in his movements, forcing an unnaturally calm manner. Miranda is explaining something with wide Latin gestures. Bardou glances at Tomlinson's and Rubikov's ghostly images in Globe 5.

His shoulders slightly hunched, Kenny stares unblinkingly at Bardou and Miranda. Cypriana's image takes shape behind Bardou; her ghostly head turns in a half circle, incredulously observing the images she sees: the conference room in Globe 14, Tomlinson, Rubikov, Kenny and the technicians. Staring at Kenny, her large eyes open wide. She struts toward him, tall, a challenging smile on her face.

"I didn't know they sent women to the Space Prison," Kenny says, startled and uncomfortable. The dark eyes come closer. Cypriana's transparent body stands inches before him, superimposed over the table. She stretches out a hand which passes through his body. Her lips move, talking soundlessly to Kenny.

"Turn on the sound," Kenny says to Rubikov. "She wants to give us a message."

"I haven't that authority," Rubikov says evasively. "There are strict orders not to contact Globe Five."

"Lee's orders?" Kenny asks with dry contempt.

"Lee's and mine." Tomlinson takes the young man firmly by the arm. "And you are going to comply. You're going to follow orders, Andrews! Or you'll be taken off your job."

Angrily Kenny frees himself from Tomlinson's grip. The phantom girl is turning, walking away from him, following Bardou and Miranda who leave the conference room in Globe 5.

"All right. Your orders, Tomlinson!" Kenny's voice is brittle with sarcasm. "But believe me, when your negotiations fail, you'll feel a moment of regret for having stopped me—a very short moment, just before we all get blown into space!"

A buzzer in Kenny's pocket purrs like a cat. Quickly Kenny fishes out a tiny transmitter.

"Andrews," he says tersely.

"This is Lee," a voice says levelly, as if disguising emotion. "Come to the control room at once."

Before Kenny can answer, the instrument shuts off. Kenny looks uncertainly at Tomlinson and Rubikov.

"Do you think he stooped so low as to listen to our conversation?" he asks.

Tomlinson chuckles. "I wouldn't put it past him!"

"How could he?" Rubikov asks, startled. "The transmitters have to be switched on before you can hear. Or he might have found a new method. . . ."

"I wouldn't put that past him either," Tomlinson says sardonically.

# XXIV

The rocket shatters the eye staring down on Cypriana and Bardou. It explodes with a dull sound, raining glass through the small room in the crew quarters. The greater part of the room is taken up by a bed. There is a built-in shower and washbasin in a corner, and a table hinged to the wall.

"I can't stand that thing spying on us," Cypriana says sharply, her olive skin flushed with anger. "I'll bet they're listening to us, too, damn them!"

Her outburst shocks Bardou out of his drowsiness, and he looks at her in surprise. Slim and straight, her karate tunic pulled taut over her small breasts, she looks wild and seductive, an Amazon unconscious of her beauty.

"Next time give me a warning before you shoot off that thing," Bardou says irritatedly. Slowly she walks over to him, sits beside him on the bed where he lies and lowers her head onto his chest.

"We've been here almost three hours," she says. "What are we waiting for?"

"They're under a lot of pressure, and it's getting worse for them every hour. I wouldn't mind sleeping a day or two."

"With me?" She puts long-fingered hands on his face, covering his eyes.

"I don't know if I'd rest much." Bardou smiles.

She moves closer and kisses him. "You're like a father to me."

"Really? Slightly incestuous, don't you think?"

"I will let you sleep, Pierre, I promise I will!"

"I know, in spurts." Bardou puts her head into the cove of his arm and strokes her soft face. Her skin smells delicately of flowers. "I know you by now."

He is afraid of her irrationality, her unpredictable explosions. He has come to understand that she turned against her father because he did not live up to the idealistic picture she had formed in her mind. Her father might have been forced to act pragmatically. Political situations demand compromises. Cypriana does not seem to understand that concept; she demands the world to conform to her desire. Anyone who does not blend into the world of hers is her enemy.

"What is it, Pierre?" she asks, taking his hand and putting it on her breast.

"Just trying to think."

"What are you going to demand from them?" she whispers close to his ear.

"Justice. Freedom. Guarantees."

"If they don't cooperate, we're going to blow up the ISC," she adds with grim anticipation. "Aren't we?"

He looks at the various ducts on the ceiling and in the walls. Any of them might hide a listening device.

"We certainly will!" he says strongly for the benefit of any invisible listeners.

"Then we'll all die together," she says with a curious pleasure.

"Yes, we'll die together," he repeats to end this conversation.

"I can't imagine any future," Cypriana complains. "Life on earth changes all the time, but on the SP nothing ever moves. What would it be like, living again like a human?"

"Everybody who's been behind bars for any length of time has been faced with that problem. You'll adjust quickly. You're young; you're only twenty."

"That's more than seven thousand days," she answers gravely, rising from the bed. She stands motionless, arrowlike, her hands clenched at her sides.

"Only seven thousand days!" he says. "I told you you could be my daughter. Maybe you are."

"You couldn't have met my mother," she answers, too tense to meet his attempt at lightness. "You were never in the Philippines. And she never left that island."

"Spiritually, I mean spiritually!" He closes his eyes wearily. He feels the heavy burden of his responsibility for the sixty people and also for the three thousand prisoners on the ISC.

Suddenly she whips around, her hand on the rocket gun. Miranda enters, followed by the rest of the committee.

"The whole general staff!" Bardou greets them with slight sarcasm. Wearily he swings his legs off the bed.

"Sorry to disturb you," Van Buren says. His angelic face with the deeply sunken vicious eyes try to smile in the frame of his long blond hair. "We decided to have a conference with you."

"We must discuss our demands," Miranda says, staring at Cypriana in ill-concealed jealousy.

"There're microphones all over the room. Do you want to cue those people in to have their answers ready?" Bardou asks.

The men squat on the floor or lean against the wall.

"I'm aware of that," Miranda answers from the floor, twisting his head to keep Cypriana in his view. "That's why we wrote down some of the points. We want you to study them. You're our spokesman, Bardou."

He holds out notes to Bardou.

"If you've discussed them, the damage has already been done. I'm not going to read them anyway; I have my own ideas. If you don't trust me, I'm ready to withdraw and you can take over, Miranda."

"That isn't our intention," Guzmán says patiently. "Of course we trust you. I composed a list of all the men and their trumped-up crimes for which they were sent to prison for life."

"If Ground insists on getting into detail, case for case, wouldn't that take weeks? I'm sure they'll settle for a general amnesty," Bardou answers.

"Amnesty," Hallstadt repeats dryly, cigarette smoke curling across his face. "Now, what would such an amnesty consist of?"

"We have a few safeguards," Bardou says. "There's no use trying to decide everything in advance. We might end up quarreling among ourselves."

"We won't," Shepilov says. His face still holds its expression of faint amusement, as though he were a spectator at a comedy. "We hold all the trumps. They hold none."

"After we make a deal, they'll have all the aces, and we'll lose our leverage," Hallstadt warns.

"It won't happen." Bardou gets up with an impatient sigh. The men do not reply, and to break the silence Bardou asks, "Where's Dubois?"

"We left him in the storeroom under guard," Van Buren says. "I still don't trust him."

"Bring him to me." Bardou walks over to the small bathroom. Closing his eyes, he turns on the water and listens to it running as if it were the sound of voices. When he turns, Cypriana stands beside him holding out a towel. Her eyes are dark with anger.

"You're taking chances," she says quietly. "If Dubois finds a way to go back to our enemies, he could tell them a lot about us."

Bardou dries his face, aware that he has to assert himself now.

"I want Dubois right away!" he orders harshly.

Van Buren grunts something under his breath, but

Hallstadt sends him out of the room with a curt movement of his head.

As Van Buren leaves, Kentu comes in breathlessly.

"They're waiting for us. The conference room is full of ghosts!"

# XXV

The sight of the green conference table transports McVeigh back to his past. An accomplished arbitrator, a con man on a global scale, McVeigh is back in his element.

Without the help of a cane he walks to the table, rejuvenated by the knowledge that he again is wanted.

McVeigh has learned that words one does not say never need be retracted later. That realization makes him, a loquacious man, taciturn in conferences.

Lee Powers approaches him to introduce a hook-nosed, white-haired man. "This is Judge Nicopulos," he says.

The judge says with Mediterranean grace, "I'm honored, Mr. President, that you've consented to conduct this meeting."

McVeigh smiles politely, not too much and not too little, just enough to keep these men in their places.

"The judge represents the law on the ISC," Lee adds, taking a seat at McVeigh's left. "The ISC's code of law is independent of any decision Ground might make."

McVeigh smiles in reminiscence. He fought the Congress and the Supreme Court and won most of the battles.

The spacejackers have made no attempt to communicate with the officials of the City in the Sky. McVeigh appreciates their shrewd strategy: Whoever takes the first step in negotiations puts himself at a disadvantage.

Two more people drift in. Names pass McVeigh's ear: Tomlinson, Rubikov, Andrews. They sit down at his end of the table, leaving the remaining part free for the holograph projections.

"Can we still talk privately?" McVeigh mutters to Lee, leaning close. He wonders at the unnatural calm Lee is showing.

"They can't hear us yet," Lee says. "The communications to Globe Five are still switched off. But we'll activate them in a few minutes."

McVeigh shifts his heavy body in his chair. His back hurts between his shoulderblades. But his heart beats in a steady, sound rhythm.

Setting down his satchel, Ingmar Bergstrom takes the chair at McVeigh's right.

"Don't you dare go sticking me with your needles!" McVeigh growls.

"You're playing with your life, Mr. President," Bergstrom answers, studying him closely to gauge his physical strength.

"This is the right moment to scare me," McVeigh says sarcastically. "I'm frightened to death! You warned me so often I'm sure I'll stay alive. Look after your lab and get me that atomic heart; that's what your job is about. Otherwise, don't bother me."

"I'd better stay around in case I'm needed," Bergstrom answers, unperturbed. "You wouldn't like having those people watch you keel over, would you?"

"No doctor likes his patient to croak in his office," McVeigh says, his mouth crooked in a smile. "Okay, stick around if it amuses you!"

Hazy shapes appear at the right and left of the table. They sharpen like pictures focusing in a camera's viewfinder. Startled, McVeigh turns to Lee to make sure his eyes aren't deceiving him.

"Holograph projection from Ground," Lee explains. "That man with the waxed mustache is Signor Mancini, present chairman of the ISC. At his side is Lefrèvre, the second-in-command of Ground. He's in Brussels."

More forms take shape until half the large table is occupied by semi-transparent projections of human beings. Some of the images overlap each other like double exposures, then slide apart as technicians separate them by adjusting the mirrors.

"Those others are government officials of the ISC corporation, representing their countries. They're Russians, Italians, Chinese—and other nations that hold shares in Space City," Lee explains. "I don't know most of them."

"My name is McClore," a grim-faced ghost announces. "I'm speaking from Ground in New York for the American government."

His face is dreamily distorted, but as the focal sharpness increases, it loses its surrounding haze. "May we elect the spokesman?" McClore suggests. His eyes search for Lee.

"Mr. McVeigh has consented to represent our group," Lee quickly answers.

"An excellent choice," Mancini concurs. "I second Dr. Powers' suggestion. Any objection?"

The group does not respond. A sudden nervousness permeates the conference room.

"From now on we can be heard in Globe Five," Lee announces. His voice carries through the microphones to the control room where Chan, Indru and Ferranti watch the television screens. "Kindly refrain from talking except when you want to be heard by the spacejackers. Ferranti! Turn on sound and picture from Globe Five."

A gray mist forms around the still-unoccupied part of the table, nebulous shapes which quickly condense into scores of human bodies. They crowd together, men in karate gowns, silent, tense, their faces marked by an implacable determination. Lee feels chilled. There is an irrationality emanating from these men, an almost visible aura of insanity.

He watches Bardou take a seat beside the group. The young woman he saw on the video screen is beside him. Her hair falls in dark, shiny tangles over half her face as though to hide her expression. To Lee she appears even more grimly determined than the others. Before her lie two of the strange rocket guns of the spacejackers. Lee's eyes meet hers, and he looks into a black pool of hatred.

McVeigh, also aware of the dark mood of these people, throws a quick glance at Lee.

The tensely packed group of spacejackers opens. Hallstadt and Van Buren accompany Dubois to the table. Dubois hesitantly sits down beside Bardou, then pulls himself together and meets the eyes of the image men in front of him as though he had cast his lot with his captors.

"Jules Dubois!" Lefrèvre exclaims, shocked. "Are you the spokesman for those people?"

Bardou answers instead. "He represents mainly your point of view." Bardou's calm face and manner contrast sharply with the people around him. "Dubois is your contact man, not ours. But by now he might be aware of our problems."

"Glad he's alive anyway," Lefrèvre says dryly.

"We have no intention of harming him," Bardou says shortly.

McVeigh shoots an angry glance at Lefrèvre, who pales, aware of his undiplomatic mistake.

"Since you've already prevented the arrival and departure of the astrocommuters for more than four hours," McVeigh says in his calm conference voice, "let's not drag out this meeting. State your demands. We're listening." He takes a pad and pencil from his pocket and puts them in front of him, then produces glasses which he balances on his long nose. "I usually work with a score of secretaries," he adds in a quiet, chatty tone to loosen the tension.

Bardou takes a piece of paper from his breast pocket and holds it up without looking at it.

"I don't need to explain the situation to you, gentlemen. But let me tell you that we are not here to make any deals. You will accept our demands. If not, the alternative is obvious to all of us. You might believe that as soon as we evacuate our position, we will be at your mercy. This isn't so. You overlooked one fact!"

His steady eyes scan the faces opposing him.

"You'll never enter the Space Prison again; that satellite will be off limits for you as long as there's life on it. The friends we left behind do not want to return to earth. You will leave provisions in its hangar. Only after the ferry has left and has returned to earth will my friends open the hangar. This is to assure us that you will live up to any agreement which will be decided between us."

"I don't know what you have in mind," McVeigh says with diplomatic ease. "Explain yourself, please."

"It doesn't need any long explanation," Dubois says. "I've been informed that in case of any betrayal by Ground, the SP will be blown up by the propellant stored to maintain its spin and orbit renewal. This explosion would endanger the orbit in which the ISC travels, damaging or even destroying the City in the Sky."

"Have you switched sides, Dubois? You seem to be working with those people," McClore says. "In any case, your threats are academic. We haven't the slightest intention of breaking our word, once we have come to an understanding. Well, let's hear your demands."

McVeigh, unhappy with the sharp tone developing between the two parties, intercedes. "Please address yourself to me, Professor Bardou. I am conducting this conference on this side. The decisions will be made by me and Judge Nicopulos."

"Then I don't see why you called in all those people," Bardou answers.

McVeigh at once realizes an advantage.

"I promise they will be quiet from here on. But they are stockholders in the ISC—their investments are at stake! Can you blame them?" He produces his famous grin which has appeased many of his adversaries. "Just ignore them—they're nothing but ghosts."

Bardou does not react to the double meaning.

"Our first demand is that the Space Prison will never be used again to incarcerate people. That unusual and brutal punishment must stop!"

"I agree with you, Professor," McVeigh answers. "And I don't think we will have difficulties in accepting this point."

"Agreed!" Mancini concurs as though he has been asked. McVeigh stares coldly above his head, to indicate that he wants Bardou to ignore the chairman of Ground.

Bardou watches the array of misty people around the table. Lightly he touches Cypriana's thigh to make sure he is not alone among phantoms. Quickly and reassuringly she puts her hand on his.

"We demand complete amnesty from every government. This includes all of us. No case should be opened again against any of my friends. There are also retractions and apologies due to many of us. Let me just mention my own case: I was arrested for having published so-called top-secret papers, agreements which were a threat to world peace, coming from a military class which in its arrogance believes itself to be omnipotent. That self-perpetuating class refuses to share any responsibility with parliaments or congresses elected by the people. For generations the military in every country has kept the world on the brink of war, to strengthen their own position. There are two constant conspiracies against mankind: The military is convinced that they are the ruling class, and they want people to put the fate of mankind in their hands. The other is in conspiracy with the military to siphon off the world's wealth."

McVeigh's expression hardens. "Are political speeches appropriate here, Professor?" he asks. His voice is flat and subdued. "Couldn't we dispose of them for the time being?"

"They explain our position, Mr. President," Bardou replies harshly. "In order to send me up for life, the military faked evidence, planting weapons in my house which they conveniently 'discovered.' I want a public apology from the French government and an unbiased investigation that can clear my name."

"Well . . ." McVeigh drawls, and his small eyes seem to sink deeper into their sockets. "If what you say is true, I don't see how anybody could stand in the way of justice. I'll see to it that your accusation is investigated, without bias."

"Not only mine. We have dozens of cases among my fellow prisoners who were railroaded into confessions by threat or torture," Bardou says heatedly.

McVeigh throws a glance across the table at the observers sent by different governments. "If you demand justice, Professor, you couldn't find a better ally than myself!"

Lowering his eyes, Bardou pretends to study the paper he is holding. McVeigh's smooth compliance arouses a mortal fear in him. What deceit are these people planning?

He looks up and scans their faces; they appear ghoulish in their transparency. Bardou singles out one he remembers.

"I see M. Alber is among the Ground's delegates. The last time I saw him was in Lyons at the trial. The judge had his consent to send me to the Space Prison.

Now I want his consent to your guarantees—his official word speaking for his government."

The man addressed as M. Alber smiles glacially. "Mr. McVeigh has our absolute consent to make any deal with you, Professor Bardou. My government will comply."

Kenny Andrews cannot control a sudden surge of impatience and fury. He has promised Lee not to talk, but his temperament breaks through his caution.

"Since you talk so much about justice, Professor, what about those people who committed crimes and were rightfully sentenced? Surely you don't want evil unconditionally rewarded—that wouldn't be the justice you want to see."

McVeigh's chest starts hurting. Bergstrom, who constantly watches him, passes a tablet to him.

"We'd better postpone this meeting," he whispers, alarmed. "Your health. . . ."

McVeigh swallows the stimulant with a big gulp of water.

"Do you want to return to your respective countries?" He stares toward Bardou but sees only a diffuse shape.

"Some of us would. But there is a group who'd like to live on an island, like Madagascar or Zanzibar."

"We would need the consent of the respective governments." McVeigh turns to the people at his right. He does not want to accept every demand without raising at least some minor obstacles.

"All this is shit," Hallstadt says quietly, flatly. "You're being taken, Bardou. These people don't have the slightest intention of sticking to their promises." His eyes glitter with hatred. "We want hostages!"

"Are you their spokesman?" McVeigh measures Hallstadt in surprise. "Who are you?"

"One of those people you want to see dead!" Hallstadt says. "I know how to deal with you, McVeigh. We want hostages delivered to Globe Five. One will be you. The second will be Lee Powers. The third one can be the chairman of a big corporation like General Motors or Krupp. And as a safeguard, a member of the Russian or Chinese politburo, too. If Ground tries any tricks, they'll die."

There is a spontaneous applause from the prisoners.

"McVeigh is in no physical condition to leave the ISC," Bergstrom objects. "I'm his doctor. He wouldn't survive a trip to earth."

"We're going to discuss your demands," McVeigh says, his voice labored.

Suddenly Miranda laughs. "I don't know what there is to discuss," he says. "Pardon my hilarity, but I just thought of something that will help you to make up your mind damned quick!"

"You'll hear from us presently," Lee says calmly, wanting to postpone any further discussion.

"I bet we will!" Miranda chuckles. He shows a row of large white teeth which change his transparent head into an ectoplasmic skull. "We'll give you fifteen minutes to deliver three hostages. Not one minute more!"

"Cut the projection, Ferranti!" Lee orders into the microphone. The images of the people in Globe 5 fade away.

"I'd better take you to your room," Bergstrom says worriedly to McVeigh. But McVeigh does not seem to hear him. He feels inadequate, unable to evaluate a situation which is clear to the scientists at the table.

"They're threatening us. What do they have in mind?"

"They have a few options." Lee has withdrawn into a stony calm. "We'll have to act fast." Alertly he turns to the faces at the table, the real and the ghostly ones. "I know how this issue can be solved."

"Right!—my way!" Kenny bursts out, jumping to his feet. "To confront those bastards only aggravates the situation. What a waste of time! They could be dead by now!"

"Violence will only make them desperate. There's a much better way," Lee states, his face tense with thought.

"What do you propose?" Mancini asks, secure in his office in Geneva. The people exposed to danger are on the ISC.

"I can't say anything just now, but I promise you that within two hours the first ferry will leave for earth," Lee says plainly as if referring to a timetable.

# XXVI

Zdeneck Svoboda quickly closes the door to his room, locks it and tries the handle for safety. Then he slumps down on the bed, his thin body curved into a circle. His thumbs snap open the attaché case. It is empty except for half a pack of cigarettes. The money is gone.

He arrived at the ISC without a change of clothes. His shirt, sweated through, clings to his slender torso.

Dully he lifts his eyes and looks toward the window with its mysterious eternal display of galaxies. The earth rises, and Svoboda numbly tries to locate the continent of Europe, Czechslovakia and Prague, his hometown. But the satellite's rotation causes the earth to move too fast for him to focus on one spot. He has the feeling he is drifting in space, turning and rolling like the ISC.

He tries to organize his thoughts. The detectives obviously had replaced the deck of cards with marked ones. How else could they have won so steadily? Even during the game he suspected that he was being cheated, but he continued to play anyway. Did they drug him? Hypnotize him? Or did he want to lose?

Svoboda is a compulsive gambler. Holding cards or throwing chips on the roulette table, he experiences that orgiastic surge of excitement which mounts and finds it climax when the ivory ball falls into the pocketed wheel or when the cards open on the green felt of the gambling table.

From his pocket Svoboda takes a small snuffbox. It contains a transparent capsule with a white powder. That powder is his secret back door escape route: he has made up his mind to die should he ever be arrested by the secret police.

Svoboda has made inquiries about death by cyanide; he was assured it would be instantaneous. The white powder is given to terminal cases in hospitals; the patient dies quickly, as though his heart were arrested by the grip of a strong hand.

"I'm only forty-two years old." He talks to himself, his voice ringing hollowly in his ears. "What did I do wrong? Where did it all fall apart?"

Since childhood he has loved to gamble—at race-tracks, at cards, with dice, making bets completely beyond his means. He gambled away his and his wife's income, and borrowed money from friends only to lose it. One day, when he returned from his office, he found his apartment empty; his wife, Jorca, had left him, taking his two children with her.

He was the treasurer of the carpenters' union and kept the union's coffers in cash in a safe, knowing that the police would confiscate any bank account the union opened. Svoboda's books were not in order. Expecting a revision of his books, he filled the attaché case with all the cash in the treasury, telling himself he could make it grow tenfold on the ISC.

Now that dream has come to an end. There is no other dream left except that of the white powder.

"Bellboy!" a voice says outside his door, and a hand knocks softly.

Warily, Svoboda approaches the door. His body feels curiously light, as if he were going to float away.

"What is it?"

"A message from Judge Nicopulos, sir."

Svoboda unlocks the door. It is pushed open viciously as though by an explosion. He is hurled backward and crashes into the foot of the bed. For a moment he lies stunned, blood oozing down his neck from a cut in his skull. As he sits up dazed, he is lifted to his feet as if he were made of cardboard.

"You don't weigh much," one detective says, while the other closes the door.

"You've got my money; leave me alone," Svoboda mutters, retreating from the man. To his surprise he puts five feet between himself and his attacker.

"We want you to come with us with the next ferry, as soon as they open the hangar," the man with the fleshy face says languidly, enjoying the situation. "They won't let you stay at the ISC if you can't pay. So you'll get a couple of years for embezzlement. Then you'll be a free man again in our free society."

Svoboda feels a curious power rising in him, a strength born of desperation and hopelessness.

"If you don't come along quietly, we'll have to ship you out of here." Though the detective is shorter by half a head, his body seems to have twice the width of Svoboda's. The second intruder produces a black nylon sack seemingly from nowhere.

Svoboda says, "All I have to do is put this pill in my mouth and bite on it. You'll have nothing but a body on your hands." Staying out of the detective's reach, Svoboda holds up the white capsule. "Then you'll be in trouble!"

"A body is easier to transport." The detective shakes his head, deploring Svoboda's misjudgment of the situation. "Go ahead. You're doing us a favor!"

"To hell with you!" Svoboda lowers his head. His right foot stemmed against the wall behind him, he suddenly shoots forward like an arrow. His head hits the man's ample stomach. The detective crashes into his companion, taking him along on his sudden flight. The two men tumble to the floor.

Svoboda pushes the door open and with a shout runs outside. He feels as if he were floating in a dream; every step takes him ten feet away from his attackers.

He turns in mid-flight to look back. The two detectives are sitting inside the door, bobbing up and down as if made of rubber.

A dog is barking frantically and shrilly. Sailing through the air toward Svoboda comes a miniature poodle, his small legs churning as though he were treading water. Behind the poodle floats a fat woman in curlers, her mouth open in an unvoiced scream.

Svoboda's body bounces against an open door, and as he catches the doorframe to steady himself, a tray heaped with dirty dishes is kicked into the air. Cutlery and glasses bounce off the walls, and small globules of water touch his cheeks softly.

A voice booms from hidden speakers: "Stay in your rooms; tie yourselves to your beds or chairs with the belts provided for this emergency. Stay in your rooms, ladies and gentlemen. We are having trouble with the gravity devices."

Desperate hands grab Svoboda and pull him close. He looks into the panicky eyes of a slender young woman. Her hair floats wildly in thick blond tresses, her sensual mouth only inches from him. Svoboda is intensely aware of the warmth of her supple body against his. He tries to remember if he took that pill—is he experiencing death in this confused tableau?

But the woman pushes him away, propelling him along the corridor, past people who hold onto handles protruding from the wall. As he touches the floor with one foot, he pushes himself forward like a sprinter. To stand still would invite death to catch up with him, death in the disguise of two fat men.

He does not know if he is walking or swimming; his long arms shoot out, pulling him forward. His body twists, and he moves along upside down, a disorienting but not uncomfortable situation.

He finds himself floating over green felt tables, and around him and turning like Christmas decorations glide the white, red, green and golden plastic chips of the gambling casino. Beginning to laugh uncontrollably, Svoboda fishes them out of the air. Blurred faces swim around him. All he wants to see and touch are the beautiful square chips which to him are life itself.

# XXVII

"Bastards! They cut us off!" Van Buren snarls.

The phantom people in Globe 5 have faded away. The spacejackers face an empty table.

Miranda looks around with a calculating expression. "I'll teach them a lesson," he announces. "Just watch me!"

Bardou's head is pounding with anger, but he manages to keep his voice low: "You just signed our death warrant, Hallstadt!"

"I did?" Hallstadt speaks with a dull anger. "You just don't know how to treat those people. You think you can get something from them by being reasonable! They'll lie to you even when they recite the Gospel! They're using you, Bardou!"

"You broke up this meeting with unreasonable demands. You didn't even give me time to lay the groundwork for a decent settlement. You slugged them. They won't take it. It was understood that I was going to conduct this conference, and you double-crossed me!" He turns to Miranda. "And you too. We had a chance to make a deal—now they know that we're fighting among ourselves. That gives them the answer!"

Cypriana puts her hand on his arm, trying to calm him. But he brushes her away and stands up.

"You're insane. All of you! I thought so when I first arrived at the SP, but I didn't want to believe it. You see life through a warped mirror. I tried to save you, but obviously you don't want to live!"

"You were catering to them!" Miranda shouts. "What happened to your smart idea? You don't know how to put it in practice. Hallstadt and I know; so does

Van Buren; so does Guzmán; so does everybody but you!"

"All right. Take over!" Bardou walks to the door, erect and cold. His zero-gravity shoes cling to the floor with slight popping noises. "You underestimate your enemy. Coercion! Hostages! You can't get away with that! They have more options than we have."

Hallstadt grimly follows Bardou.

"I agree with Miranda—only force produces results. You still think like those people. You don't belong with us, Bardou."

Bardou walks on, unwilling to listen. Did he really believe he could carry out a complex, dangerous mass escape with these lunatics?

Hallstadt says, "Don't worry, I thought ahead. I posted guards at every air shaft, every trapdoor, every plate that can be removed. If they try to sneak in here, they'll get killed. I know they have better weapons. But if we lose, I'll smash the control panel—that'll finish the ISC."

"We're going to blow up the ISC!" Cypriana says in her airy, girlish voice. "That'll be our salvation and our freedom. We'll create a historic reminder for generations to come. Injustice will be punished! Our death will make a better world."

"I wanted you to live," Bardou says sadly, looking at her as if to imprint her picture in his mind forever. "Blow up the ISC and three thousand people will die with you. I don't see how that can bring justice to any world."

Cypriana's face is lit by a strange ecstasy, like a martyr yearning for the stake.

"I love you," she whispers, stepping close to him. "Are you going to betray me like my father?"

Bardou shakes his head. "You chose the road of no return; it leads nowhere. Your father knew better than that, at least. But you never understood him, any more than you understand me!"

He enters the control room with its banks of panels. Computer lights travel in staccato flashes. He feels Miranda close behind him.

"Watch me! I'll show you how they'll come around to our demands and even thank us for it!"

The two crewmen of the ISC in their soft-colored overalls scatter as Miranda, his hands outstretched like claws, jumps between them. "You want nonviolence? Okay, this is nonviolence!" In quick succession he depresses a row of switches. "All we have to do to make those bastards show up here is stop the rotation of the ISC!"

The six small rockets on top of Globe 6 which spin the huge mass of the International Space City around its axis stop firing. The counterjets on top of Globe 8, on the opposite side of the satellite, come to life. White streams of vapor shoot into the black void, and the entire satellite slowly comes to a standstill.

Bardou feels light-headed, a quick euphoria flooding his mind. Van Buren springs up, lifting himself birdlike off the floor, flapping his arms and bouncing back softly, his face of an unearthly beauty. With a dancer's graceful leap he reaches Hallstadt and embraces him, pressing his cheek against his friend's.

"I don't know why we should die!" He laughs. "You won't permit me to die! Will you, Hans?"

Holding his breath, Hallstadt pushes him away and looks around like a cornered animal. His face contorts as he attempts painfully to think clearly.

"Something's happening . . . something . . ." he mutters.

Bardou turns a full circle in midair. The faces flitting past his vision seem to have doubled in number. Their expressions have changed to radiant smiles, and voices break the stillness, punctuated only by the click of computers, until they become thunder in Bardou's ears.

Kentu sinks to the floor in an attitude of prayer, lifting up his face in ecstasy, his dark throat moving in convulsive laughter. Dubois enters the control room but dissolves in front of Bardou's eyes into an indistinct shape.

"Gas!" Hallstadt shouts. "They're blowing gas through the air vents!" He coughs and tries to breathe through his fingers.

"Happy gas!" It is Shepilov's voice, gay, amused.

Bardou fights to clear his mind; he knows this euphoria can mean death for them all.

"Nitrous oxide!" Behrmann shouts, his consciousness slipping into a velvety darkness.

Hallstadt looms in front of Bardou's unfocused vision; he looks like a row of men. They carry weapons lifted high above their heads. Iron bars? Axes? Bardou cannot make them out. That platoon of Hallstadts moves in unison, mechanical men activated by the same spring. The elation in Bardou changes to terror.

The Hallstadt figures lift their weapons higher to smash them into the blinking, scurrying computer lights.

Bardou jumps at Hallstadt and grabs him by the throat; the two of them sail toward the ceiling of the control room. They hit the curved roof and bounce away in a deadly embrace. Hallstadt's head strikes the floor, and the ax slips out of his hands. Bardou presses Hallstadt's throat. The surge of elation returns in him, a euphoria that surges through every muscle in his body.

He discovers Cypriana standing over him, a slim, tall Amazon. She is gripping two rocket guns. A golden glow seems to emanate from her. Time freezes in Bardou's mind. He watches two finned rockets crawl out of the barrels, driving inexorably toward him. He tries to move out of their path, but his body is welded to Hallstadt's.

Bardou feels a numbing impact as the shafts bore into his chest.

Laughter is rising to a crescendo, numbing his ears. Cypriana's face bends over him, and in her eyes he discovers infinity. From all sides men without faces descend. They are wearing masks with trunks. His fading sense of hearing registers almost soundless explosions.

A deep calm permeates his body. He sinks willingly into soft blackness.

# XXVIII

"How much nitrous oxide do we have on board?" Lee asks the engineers in the monitor room.

Tomlinson immediately grasps the thought behind Lee's question. He activates the videophone connecting him with Rubikov.

"Nitrous oxide? What's that?" McVeigh, sitting in a wheelchair Bergstrom has procured for him, feels inadequate. As President he was always wary of scientists; he did not understand their world, and he could never trust their ideas.

"It's a soporific," Bergstrom says. "It puts people to sleep."

"Ah!" McVeigh's strained features become lively with excitement. Pushing Bergstrom away, he gets up. "A stroke of genius, Powers! You only live for your moments of excellence! Then you rise!"

Impatiently Lee switches on banks of monitors. Their projections change rapidly, focusing on the interior of Globe 5, the storerooms, crew quarters, control rooms, the hangar with its catwalks and gangs of armed men patrolling aimlessly. A confused muddle of voices rises and subsides as the projections vary.

Kenny's face is rigid with surprise. "Of course! That's what has to be done! Why didn't I think of it?"

"Rubikov has enough to gas up the ISC," Tomlinson reports.

"Tell him to connect the nitrous oxide containers with the oxygen intake leading to Globe Five. He should start with five cc's concentration and increase it to twenty-five cc's per cubic foot. Kenny, put gas masks on your men; be ready to attack Globe Five in eight minutes. I'll give the order."

His frustrations vanishing, Kenny flies out of the monitor room.

"Intelligent of you not to inform Ground," McVeigh says in admiration. "Those idiots would have insisted on a unanimous decision."

Lee turns to Bergstrom. His voice is clipped. "How much nitrous oxide does a body absorb safely?"

"The body reacts almost instantaneously, but the gas won't become toxic before ten minutes' intake." Bergstrom forces McVeigh back into his chair. "Let me take you to your room, Mr. President."

"Crap," McVeigh mutters, but sits down obediently. "I wouldn't miss this show if it were the last in my life!"

He looks at the kaleidoscopic change of projections. Some, where the lenses have been shot out, stay blank; others light up sharply. Fascinated, McVeigh watches the activities in Globe 5, the lightly packed crowd milling about. Sounds and snatches of conversation overlap unintelligibly.

"Rubikov should add the gas slowly," Tomlinson advises. "Increased pressure in the valves produces hissing noises. Some of those people are technicians; they'd become suspicious."

"If they do, we might lose the game." Lee searches for Bardou on one of the monitor screens. Discovering him at the atomic control panel, he moves in with the zoom lens. Bardou's face is drawn, desperate.

"Shut off all sounds except those in the control room," Lee orders Ferranti.

Ferranti turns off the audio projections except for the brilliantly lit room with its banks of computer panels in Globe 5.

Rubikov is at Lee's side.

"Your cc estimate is too low, Powers. I started with ten cc's. The load will have to be increased to fifty if you want to knock them out fast."

"You're the biochemist," Lee mutters. "How long until they fall asleep?"

"Not very quickly," Rubikov answers worriedly. "They'll soon lose coordination and become delirious, though. You should have used a lethal gas that would work more efficiently."

"And kill our crew in Globe Five?" Lee grunts.

"Better to have twenty-two men die than endanger three thousand."

Kentu's dark head fills one of the monitor screens. His muscular frame collapses; his face turns up sharply as though his neck were broken. He screams with hysterical laughter. Miranda steps over him, brandishing his rocket gun. There is insanity in his wide eyes. Van Buren's blurred figure comes onto the screen, then his body drifts out of sight toward the ceiling of the control room.

A premonition grips Lee. "Turn on all sounds!" he shouts over his shoulder to Ferranti. "Activate all monitors fully!"

Screams and laughter rise from a crowd of men in the storeroom. Some embrace each other, whirling in a dervish's dance, faster and faster until their images blur. Canned food thrown from the storeroom hits the dancers, knocking them off their feet; they crash into the walls. In the crew quarters Jules Dubois takes shelter in the shower and closes the door. A man brandishes a rocket gun and, screaming, fires it, his eyes shut. A human head floats past the screen, distorted in petrified laughter. The fins of a rocket missile protrude from his forehead.

"They're losing their minds!" McVeigh exclaims, fascinated. "They're completely out of control!"

A voice rings out, higher in sound than the others, sharper in its terror:

"Gas!" Hallstadt is shouting.

Lee watches Hallstadt break the glass of a box with

fire-fighting equipment. He grabs an ax and with two enormous strides passes Bardou. He swings the ax at the computer that controls the atomic panel.

Without taking his eyes off Bardou, Lee shouts, "Kenny, break into Globe Five! Don't wait! Break in!" Shorts in the wrecked computer would cause an explosion in the atomic reactor that might tear the ISC apart.

Bardou suddenly flies at Hallstadt, and grabs Hallstadt's throat. The two men shoot upward, turning in midair, writhing, welded into one body. They float so close to the monitor's screen that it seems they will smash into it. Hallstadt gasps for breath, his hands still clasped around the ax handle. Bardou hangs from his neck. They crash to the floor.

Then Lee sees Cypriana stride forward. Brandishing two rocket guns, she fires them into Bardou's body. Blood spouts up, shooting through the control room in globules, darting back and forth as though they had life of their own.

Their faces protected with gas masks, Kenny's men storm the room. Kenny brandishes a club to knock out Miranda, but he misses him. His powerful thrust whirls him helplessly in the zero gravity of the control room.

But Miranda's gun is not pointed at him. With a deep moan Miranda fires a rocket into the back of the young woman's head. Her black luxurious hair explodes; the skull breaks open, releasing a cascade of blood and brain fragments that splash through the air and mix with the globules of Bardou's blood. They circle each other like tiny planets.

# XXIX

The gravity jets on top of Globe 6 start spouting vapor, and the giant, cumbersome satellite resumes its rotary motion. Gravity slowly returns to the outer globes of the ISC. It takes twenty minutes of jet propulsion to get the mass of seventy-four thousand tons revolving around its axis.

The floating objects and drops of liquid inside the Space City settle softly on tables, chairs, beds and floors. Sanitary crews work quickly with vacuum cleaners to suck up moisture, their warm airstream evaporating the humidity. In the casino croupiers collect cards, gambling chips and dice, locking them back in their coffers. Barmen retrieve bottles and carefully pluck glasses out of the air.

Robaire has not left his office since the crisis began. Now he turns his attention to the next pressing problem: how to calm the hotel guests.

His private butler, Ovidio, serves him his favorite drink: champagne seasoned with maraschino and aged port.

"Stay with me, Ovidio," Robaire says. "I need assurance. I have to give a speech to my skittish guests, to convince them not to run away with the next ferry." He checks his face in the mirror one final time. "Do I look all right? You know, guests are like women men are trying to make. One wrong word, one false intonation, too much eagerness, and they drift off."

"You certainly don't look a day older than thirty," Ovidio says, his face creased in a compassionate grin. "Even *madre mia* would not give you more years than perhaps thirty-five!"

"Thank you," Robaire says. "Wish me good luck!" He switches on the videophone and talks to the operator. "Connect me with every video transmitter in the hotel. Flash the emergency signal in every room. Then, when you have the connections, switch me on." He smiles at Ovidio, pleased by the young man's statuesque physique.

The green light flashes on Robaire's videophone.

"Ladies and gentlemen." Robaire looks straight into the camera. "This is your host, Marcel Robaire, speaking. As you have discovered, normal operations have been restored in the International Space Hotel. I hope the temporary lack of gravity hasn't inconvenienced you too much. It was an amusing experience, don't you agree? Though the excitement is over, please stay in your rooms for the moment. It is not necessary to use the gravity belts any longer. Our well-trained crew will clean up should there be any spillage or breakage. Our excellent organization will work for you as smoothly as always.

"I hope you will stay on a long time enjoying our comforts. There will be a special event tonight at the great ballroom: the election of Miss Space. Twenty-five most beautiful women from all over the world will compete for the honor of being named Miss Space, the queen of the galaxies. Your vote will help decide that choice. We've also ordered two special orchestras from earth for your enjoyment. Free drinks will be served, and the casino will hand every guest one hundred ISC dollars in gambling chips as our small compensation for any inconvenience you might have suffered during the emergency. What could be more pleasurable than winning a fortune at the table with money received for free?"

Robaire's carefully made-up face folds into a boyish grin. "So please accept our deepest apologies. If you have any wish we can fulfill, please don't hesitate to inform your bell captain. He is, as I am, your obedient servant. The International Space Hotel thanks you and its management is looking forward with pleasure to greeting you tonight at the Miss Space Pageant."

His white teeth flashing, he stares steadily into the videophone. He once read that baring one's teeth is an atavistic remnant of the caveman, intended to frighten aggressors. Robaire feels that prehistoric urge; secretly he hates guests, their demanding unconcern, their crudeness and lack of grace, shortcomings for which they can compensate only by spending money. But how many guests have been alienated by the disaster? There might be a stampede, an exodus.

Robaire darkens the video screen.

"Did my message go over?" He turns anxiously to Ovidio.

"If I were a guest listening to you, I wouldn't leave the ISC. Announcing the Miss Space Contest was a stroke of genius! Wasn't that scheduled for the day after tomorrow?"

"It was, but it just occurred to me during my talk that a flesh show might convince a lot of people to stay. Now I'll have to convince that old bitch Signora Barracini, who chaperones the girls. I bet she'll blackmail me!"

"You can handle her," Ovidio answers politely. Robaire nods and gives him permission to leave.

He is alone. His face collapses. A shudder runs through his body, an aftertremor of fear. He unlocks a drawer and takes out a hypodermic needle which he carefully fills from an ampule. Injecting the drug in his arm, he watches his face in the mirror coming back to life. The skin tightens; his eyes regain their vigor. Robaire hides the hypodermic and locks the drawer.

Signora Barracini, the dowager in charge of the Miss Space aspirants, is still in bed with Bichon, her Sealyham terrier. During the zero-gravity period Bichon had drifted away, barking in terror and treading the air as if it were water. Signora Barracini retrieved the floating animal. How she found her way back to her room and bed, she does not recall. Still wearing the safety belt around her ample midriff, she does not trust Robaire's announcement and hides Bichon under her bedsheet. Bichon stops whimpering and falls asleep. The dog's snoring convinces Signora Barracini that the emergency is over, or Bichon wouldn't have relaxed.

A servant with a large vacuum cleaner enters, followed by two maids in miniskirts, their long legs prettily covered with silver stockings. The servant bows ceremoniously. "*Permesso!*" he says in Italian, a word incongruent to his Polynesian face. The man disappears into the bathroom. There the toilet has ejected its contents. The two maids work with great dexterity and speed, picking up drifting objects: jewelry, Signora's hairpiece, her clothes and shoes, Bichon's ruby collar and many small bottles with perfume and makeup. One of the maids passes Signora's dentures discreetly to her. Her teeth restored, Signora smiles at the young girls.

The room clean, the bathroom disinfected, the maids and the Polynesian leave. As soon as she is alone, Signora swings her legs out of bed and uncovers Bichon.

"We had a bad time, Bichon, didn't we?" She puts on a gown and fixes her face in the mirror. She still feels the weightless buoyancy of the past hour, and in retrospect it does not seem to have been so unpleasant. The incident might be to her advantage, she muses. Robaire is acting without her consent in announcing the Miss Space Pageant for tonight. She understands Robaire's dilemma, but it creates an opportunity for her that she will not pass up.

She knows he will have to call her and as soon as she thinks of this, the video screen on the wall hums softly.

Robaire's handsome face appears as she turns on the viewer. He looks at her with humility.

"Signora Barracini, I must talk with you!"

"You should have talked with me before you made that announcement," the dowager answers the screen, producing a valise which she begins to pack.

"You won't leave me!" Robaire cries.

"Do you expect me to stay after all that horror I and my poor girls have gone through?"

"But everything is normal again." Robaire's voice is tightly controlled, a fact not lost on her. "You have a contract with the ISC to stay until Miss Space has been elected. We need you."

"That is your problem," Signora says unmoved, caressing Bichon as the dog crawls into her lap. Mentally she is calculating how much money she might force the Space Hotel to pay her to stay. "We'll leave with the first ferry," she says.

"You want money, don't you?" Robaire says coldly.

"Well, if you want those frightened girls to stay, you'll have to make it worth their while."

"Don't take advantage of a man who's in trouble," Robaire pleads. "It is beneath you, signora."

"When I was young, dear M. Robaire, I believed money was terribly important in life. As I grew older, I found that I was right."

Robaire sighs. "All right. I will give you five thousand francs and each of the girls a bonus of five hundred."

"French or Swiss?"

"French."

"The Swiss franc is higher."

"Then Swiss," Robaire consents smoothly. Now that he has established she can be bribed all that is left is to fix the amount.

But Signora Barracini is not finished. "Since this is

so important to you, I think you should make my share twenty thousand Swiss francs."

"I'll make it ten," Robaire counters. "Fifteen if I don't have to pay the girls anything."

"How unfair to them!" Signora says indignantly. "But I accept."

"French francs."

"Swiss, and I want the money within an hour."

"I'll send you a check," Robaire says, trying his last ruse.

"Cash," Signora says, surprised that he underestimates her intelligence. "I won't give you an opportunity to blackmail me later with a canceled check!"

"I don't know who is blackmailing whom!" Robaire grumbles.

"Blackmail is a harsh word, M. Robaire," Signora counters with a smile. "At my age, one does not need youth, or beauty, or character. What a woman like me needs is cold cash!"

# XXX

Noiselessly Lee closes the door to his apartment, shutting out the turmoil of the past hours.

Susanne Lesuer lies on his bed in her leotards, her tangled shiny hair flowing to the floor. The gravity belt is tightened over her flat hips; her black lashes lie on her cheeks like painted shadows. Lee watches her motionlessly, breathing quietly in order not to wake her.

The soles of his shoes, adhesive to the floor, emit a tiny, sucking noise. As he steps closer, his mind pushes the terror of the last hours into a misty past. He wants to touch her hair, but his hand stops an inch away.

Susanne's hands seem startlingly white and two-dimensional in contrast with her black leotard; her nails are kept short, as though she were used to working with her hands. Her feet are bare, the toes long and supple, the balls of her dancer's feet calloused. Her small breasts move in slow, relaxed rhythm, and her face is vividly alive even in its deep sleep.

Lee wants to touch her, but he hates to shorten this quiet moment. He kneels beside her and watches her sleep, feeling a deep peace settling over him.

As though some vibration has touched her senses, the dense curtain of the girl's lashes lifts, and her light eyes slowly return from sleep.

"I didn't want to fall asleep," she says softly. "Did I sleep long?"

"Some time," he whispers.

"How long?"

She lies motionless; only her eyes and lips move.

"Does it matter?"

"It does. We've lost time."

Pushing back her hair with one hand, she sits up. Her other hand opens and she looks at the stone from Mercury which she has been holding.

"It's mine, isn't it?"

"You can have the whole damn planet." He grins. "And if you want more, just ask for it. You can have the galaxy with all the stars and suns and planets and black holes and quasars and pulsars. Just name it, you get it!"

She studies him earnestly. "You look exhausted," she says, disturbed by his drawn features.

"I'm all right. A shower and fresh clothes, and I'll be in shape again."

"You keep whispering. Is somebody listening?"

"Sound is an intruder," he says, and touches her face with the tip of his fingers. "Sound is like a third person. We don't want anybody else around, do we?"

"No." She sits up straight, fluid and alive. "But what time is it anyway? I never wear a watch. I don't like anything on my body to weigh me down. And I don't have any conception of time. You wouldn't believe it, but when I'm working, I truck an old train engineer's watch around with me, to make sure I won't miss being on time."

"You slept for almost five hours," Lee says.

"You were away that long?"

"Yes." Suddenly the strain of the past hours returns to him. "I'd better take a shower. Do you mind? I bet I smell."

She smiles warmly. "You take that shower, and I'll pick out a shirt for you from your closet."

Still clenching the Mercury rock in one hand, she opens the gravity belt with the other. The sudden movement of her body propels her up. Not used to the effect of zero gravity, she lets out a small cry of surprise. Quickly Lee catches hold of her, snatching her out of the air. Her body is small in his hands, a soft presence fusing with his.

"I won't fly away!" she says with a girlish giggle. "But if you don't hurry, I will!"

"All right! The shower! Find me a shirt, please, and a pair of gray pants."

He lowers her onto the bed.

"Socks too? Where are they?"

"This room has no secrets except you," he whispers, and enters the tiny bathroom with its basins and shower. He removes his shirt, which is drenched with perspiration. His face in the mirror looks lined, his eyes tired. Lee strips naked, yearning for the hot stream of vapor that will wash away the tension of the last hours.

He turns on the shower, and jets of pressurized water envelope him. In the reduced gravity, the water that drips from his body forms into drifting globules; a ventilator sucks them up.

The fluid hits his body sharply and pleasantly from all sides. One jet shoots out liquid, choreographed in a precise spray-soap-wash cycle. It runs in rivulets on his body toward the sucking air vent in the ceiling.

Thoughts which he tried to shut out again penetrate his consciousness. His mind clicks into computerized logic, evaluating the situation in the ISC. Globe 5 has been reoccupied; Kenny directed that phase of the attack without bloodshed. Robaire is placating the passengers and guests. Bergstrom is looking after the patients in the hospital, many of whom probably don't even know there was an emergency. Mancini, Lefrèvre and members of the corporation of the City in the Sky will surely show up with the first ferries. Nicopulos is going to arbitrate with the prisoners. The Space Prison has to be contacted, to prevent another disaster. But that phase of the development still leaves a time of grace.

Shutting his eyes, he moves closer to the water jet,

droplets like small bullets massage his forehead, his cheeks, his mouth. He holds his breath, enjoying the prickly waterstream as it explodes on his skin.

Then he feels a body against his, a body which touches him lengthwise from his knees to his chest, clinging, pressing. Opening his eyes, he sees a wave of black hair swirling around his face. The sound of the vapor jets softens the echo of laughter.

Lee turns off the faucets. At once the curtain of shiny hair sinks down, revealing Susanne's face spread in a puckish grin.

"I need a shower, too," she says, and turns the water on again. "You don't mind if I share the shower with you?" The suction of the vent above draws tiny planets of water across her cheeks. They ascend, rolling off her forehead to float higher, rushing into the egress.

"It's the first law of the ISC to save water," he says, looking down at her bare shoulders, the hard breasts, the flat dancer's stomach, the triangular black island of hair, an exclamation mark in the white softness of her skin. "You should be congratulated for having caught the spirit of Space City so quickly."

"I was lonely," she confesses. "I couldn't wait any longer."

Her body is jewellike in its perfection. Long subtle dancer's arms move to his neck. She lifts her mouth against his.

"I want you to make love to me," she says, floating up to his face. "Hold me tight and make love to me." She bends her head back in laughter, her white throat close to his mouth. "How does a man know he should make love to a girl if she doesn't tell him?"

Her straightforwardness makes it easy for him to return her embrace, sweeping away all thoughts from his mind. Locked together, they float out of the tiny bathroom into his bedroom.

There is an eternity in the bodies of two people, an ultimate destiny, an infinity of existence. Fusing with her into one entity, Lee loses track of where his body ends and hers begins. Their movements are light; suspended in midair, they turn, slowly propelled by their rhythmic movements. A golden flame runs through their bodies, corporal, corporeal, pressing them tighter to each other. Small dikes in Lee's brain give way, and a deep, boundless peace is flooding his mind.

"This is the universe," she says, her eyes regaining focus, her body obedient to his. "It's a dance—my dance, your dance. This is what dancing is about."

"It's fate." He talks into the intimacy of her taunting smile. They laugh as their weight resiliently hits the bed.

"Something new for me, making love in midair! Is it for you too?" Tears of laughter flow sideways out of her eyes. With a wild, uncontrolled strength she throws herself on Lee, and kisses him savagely, like an animal in attack.

Lee again feels a tension rising in him, challenged by her untamed ferocity.

She clings to him, her small frame soft, pliable, her breath close to his face.

"We should rent out rooms for people who want to make love in zero gravity," she says, her voice is a mixture of words and laughter. "We would make a fortune! Making love in bed can be hard on the woman. But in midair. . . !"

Playfully she covers his face with her hair and searches for his lips under the cover of that soft dark curtain.

"Don't suffocate me, I still have things to do!" he gasps.

She lifts herself up on her arms and looks at him with curiosity. At once he feels lonely as she passes out of his close range. Her face breaks into a mischievous grin.

"Now I know why you're so famous as an inventor! You really have new and revolutionary ideas!"

"When I'm challenged by a problem, I have to solve it," he says, his hand stroking her elegant back. "It's an idiosyncrasy."

"Am I a problem?" she asks with a sigh.

He does not answer but passes his hand over her face, lightly touching her mouth.

"Am I?" she breathes between his fingers.

"Quiet," he says softly.

"What are you thinking about?" Susanne asks, lifting a subtle leg and moving it in a dance.

"How to put zero gravity in my chalet in Thun."

"You have a house in Switzerland?"

"At the Lake of Thun, at the foot of the Alps."

"And you want to make gravity disappear in your bedroom, maybe by turning a switch?"

"No. By holding you."

"We couldn't do that all the time!" She pulls away, covering her small breasts with her arms in sudden chastity.

"We could try. That is, if you'll come to see me."

"Of course, I will if I ever have a vacation. You know, I'm booked up for months."

"Well. One has to do whatever's more important. Dancing for you has priority above anything else. I understand."

"What you're doing also has priority in your life. You're not much different. I know you by now."

"You do?"

"How could I miss? You're a dancer, too—a dancer of ideas." She kisses him slowly, lingeringly. She says, "I'd like to live with you, quietly. No appointments, no contracts, no travels from country to country." She stops, frowning.

"Let's live together," Lee says, yearning for her. "Let's live through one day, just one day, and then just the next day, and go on and on. Soon that drive to go and go and go will evaporate from our minds, and we might become happy and contented."

"Let's try that!" she says happily. "I'll visit you in Thun at your chalet, and stay and stay and stay and never travel again."

"When?"

Her face suddenly becomes somber. "Soon, very soon," she says as she looks into his eyes. "You are my dance, my command performance!"

# XXXI

The decompressors start their staccato rhythm, pumping out the air in the hangar until it matches the vacuum of space. The door leading to the void opens like the iris of a giant eye. Astrocommuter VIP, Ground's most luxurious spacecraft, reserved for the directors of the City in the Sky, glides into its mooring. At once the iris shuts out the darkness outside and air rushes through hundreds of vents into the hangar. The door leading to the innards of the ISC slides open: Kenny rides in in a small passenger train.

"Landing completed," the engineer in the control booth announces through the loudspeakers. The door of the astrocommuter opens.

A dozen men emerge rapidly, carrying automatic rifles and submachine guns. Rehearsed for the commando raid, they scan catwalks, post themselves at doors, dominating the hangar with their guns.

Stunned by the unexpected attack, Kenny watches the intruders. Mancini, followed by Lefrèvre, steps out of the astrocommuter. Kenny regains his equilibrium and approaches Mancini.

"What's this supposed to mean?" he demands.

"We just tested your security precautions, Andrews, you're incapable of safeguarding the ISC," Mancini says tensely. "Ground decided to take over your duties."

"You can't bring armed men with you!" Kenny protests.

"We just did! Signor Mancini ordered me to take over the security of the ISC. You're fired, Andrews," Lefrèvre barks at him.

"You have no jurisdiction up here," Kenny says coldly. "Are you thinking of trying any shooting?"

Mancini looks toward the door, where a cluster of Kenny's security force has assembled, armed with tear-gas bombs and automatic weapons; they look strange and inhuman behind their gas masks. The engineers in the control booth quickly close the shatterproof door.

Mancini watches with apprehension as more and more security guards spill into the hangar.

"I want your men back in the ferry immediately, Mancini," Kenny says, a hidden threat in his voice.

"Signor Mancini is the ultimate authority of the International Space City!" Lefrèvre blusters.

"I am taking my orders from Dr. Powers," Kenny says with cold patience. "Half a dozen people have died here in the last few hours—do you want to add some more?"

"Are you threatening us?" Lefrèvre asks angrily.

"I certainly am." The two men lock eyes. Lefrèvre finally averts his.

"We came up here to protect the ISC."

"I've already taken precautions, as you can see." Kenny feels a deep dislike for Lefrèvre; to him Lefrèvre is just one more policeman, and Kenny saw more than enough of them in his youth.

"You don't seem to be doing a good job," Mancini says.

"You want me to act according to my authority?" Kenny answers. "All right. You and your men are under arrest!"

Mancini turns to Lefrèvre as if blaming him for the situation.

"You'll have to explain your actions to Judge Nicopulos," Kenny says.

Mancini presses his lips together and with a pompous authority tries to enter the train.

Kenny stands in front of him, barring his way. "We

don't leave until your men are in the ferry," he announces.

"Are you trying to give me orders?" Mancini flares up.

"Yes," Kenny replies curtly. "I'll bring charges against both of you for assault with deadly weapons!"

Lefrèvre watches more security men stream into the hangar, outnumbering his guards. "We'll talk about that when we see the judge."

Kenny points at the telescopic lenses attached to the video screens above the hangar's doors.

"You're on record, Lefrèvre; your arrival has been taped. Now I want this hangar cleared! The ferry will return immediately to earth with your guards in it."

"All right, all right," Mancini mutters, defeated. "Lefrèvre, send them back!" He enters the train.

"You just killed your future promotion!" Lefrèvre says under his breath as he passes Kenny.

There is an oppressive silence between the three men. Kenny watches the guards from Ground retreat into the astrocommuter.

The train starts to move, turning like a turtle, leaving the hangar. "Those prisoners are to be sent back to earth," Mancini announces, trying to establish authority.

"That's up to Judge Nicopulos to decide," Kenny says dismissively.

The train, rolling on adhesive tires through a twenty-foot-high spoke toward Globe 4, passes a first-aid hospital, storerooms, machine shops for repair and modification of instruments.

"I want to talk to Powers immediately!" Mancini says angrily.

"You will, you will."

The train enters Globe 4 and stops. Elevators lead to ten rows of corridors. The globe, one hundred feet high, is lighted from hidden sources. With its honeycombed spans, it has the appearance of a giant beehive. Globe 4 contains the apartments for scientists, the crew and the hotel quarters for visitors from Ground.

Kenny steps out of the train, followed by Mancini and Lefrèvre.

"Gravity one," Mancini observes with a smile, hoping to get back on more friendly footing with Kenny. "That weightlessness makes me edgy." He freezes as Kenny opens the door to the courtroom. Fifty hostile faces of men in karate gowns stare at him—the inmates from the Space Prison. Some are resting on benches, others on the floor, quiet, tense and dangerous-looking.

"This way to the judge's chamber." Kenny walks calmly ahead, Mancini and Lefrèvre close behind. To show their contempt, the SP men don't move out of the way. Mancini, stepping over bodies, feels that he's running a gauntlet.

"Why don't you post guards around these men?" Lefrèvre mutters to Kenny.

"Those people are not aggressive at this time. They are waiting for a decision," Kenny says quietly. "And as you know, I needed my security guards in the hangar."

They enter a room paneled like a library in an old English castle.

"Those savages are killers!" Lefrèvre raises his voice now that he feels safe. "You had a good chance to get rid of them when they were drugged. We wouldn't have asked any questions!"

"Violence is against Dr. Powers' orders," Kenny says.

"You should have told that to the spacejackers!" Lefrèvre says sarcastically. "Did Powers decree that things which are unlawful can't happen? I don't know who's the bigger menace to the ISC, him or those criminals!"

Nicopulos, with his sleek white hair and his assured face, enters from the door behind the large Georgian writing desk. Lee and Tomlinson are with him.

"We watched your surprising arrival, Signor Mancini. We fail to comprehend your action," Nicopulos says with a politeness that carries a threat.

"I should think my purpose was self-evident," Mancini says, glowering in an attempt to assert his authority. "My job is to protect a three-hundred-billion-dollar investment. You have been neglecting your duty! You're taking a great risk by not locking up those desperate characters."

He sits down belligerently, staring at Nicopulos, waiting for an explanation.

"You don't seem to be aware of the ISC's constitution," says Nicopulos, "even though I believe you helped devise it."

Mancini laughs harshly. "I didn't come up here to argue. Those people will be shipped out, by force if necessary. The courts on earth will decide their destiny."

Lee sits down beside the judge and Tomlinson.

"We are the prisoners, Mancini."

"What are you talking about?" Mancini demands. "You have them rounded up in the courtroom."

"A solution can only be arrived at by careful negotiations," Tomlinson says. "If that is still possible!"

"Of course it's possible!" Lefrèvre says heatedly. "Turn over the situation to me, and I'll solve it without any further discussion!"

"All right, you talk to the leaders of those men," Nicopulos says. He produces a long, thin Russian cigarette and lights it ceremoniously. "Andrews, please call in their spokesmen. We'll give the chairman of the ISC the courtesy of making the decision."

Kenny walks to the door.

"I understand that I now have the irrevocable authority to resolve this dilemma." Mancini quickly takes advantage of Nicopulos's offer.

"Absolutely," Nicopulos agrees. "The responsibility rests fully with you."

Kenny returns with Guzmán, Behrmann and Shepilov.

"You know Signor Mancini and M. Lefrèvre," Nicopulos says. "They're going to help us arrive at a mutually satisfactory agreement."

"I remember the gentlemen faintly," Guzmán says, smiling easily. "Or should I say—transparently?"

"You represent those men out there?" Lefrèvre asks, his face hard.

"We're only their spokesmen," Shepilov answers. "Whatever is decided here has to be approved by our friends."

Mancini shakes his head in disbelief. Is he witnessing some farce? Powers and Nicopulos treating condemned murderers as equals!

"We shall present our demands to you," Behrmann says.

"Demands!" Lefrèvre explodes. "What gives you the right to demand? You were criminals even before you attacked the ISC and endangered three thousand lives!"

"I don't see any reason for concessions," Mancini adds grimly. "You lost, Guzmán. You and your people will be brought to justice."

"This looks like a wake where the corpse is missing," Shepilov says with a taunting grin. "Do you want to play the corpse, Signor Mancini?"

"What is all this?" Mancini has the impression that he is surrounded by insanity.

"You can't send those men either to the Space Prison

or to earth without their consent," Lee says softly.

"I'd like to know what could stop me," Mancini says belligerently, his eyes darting from face to face.

The video screen on the wall lights up and blinks in short flashes.

"Dr. Powers." Gay Chan's voice comes from the speaker. "We contacted the Space Prison. Vera Stern is ready to speak with Signor Mancini."

"Why should I talk to her?" Mancini asks irritatedly.

"As it happens," Guzmán says, "she's the one in a position to decide for all of us."

# XXXII

Ingmar Bergstrom, carrying a small tray covered with gauze, enters the hospital room. With slow, storklike steps he approaches McVeigh's bed. He puts the box on the table next to McVeigh as carefully as if it were made of a spider's web.

"You look good," he says approvingly, his trained ear measuring McVeigh's breathing, silently evaluating his patient's condition.

"Here I is and I don't know where I are," McVeigh jokes feebly. "What did you bring me? A gin and tonic under wraps?"

"Have a look at it. You might never see it again, except perhaps on X rays."

With a gloved hand Bergstrom lifts the veil to reveal an odd-shaped object that has little similarity to a human heart except for the seven inlets and outlets for the arteries.

McVeigh studies the gadget without visible interest. "My future heart?"

"It should serve you a hundred years," Bergstrom replies cheerfully. "A few days' rest and you'll be strong enough for the transplant. A week later you'll hop out of bed like a twenty-year-old."

McVeigh does not react; his mind is on another subject.

"Powers quit. Judge Nicopulos called me; he wants to talk to me. I think he wants to offer me the position as the head of the International Space City."

"An excellent idea!" Bergstrom's smile is broad. "A very good solution to his problems! And to yours too, Mr. President, since you won't be able to leave the ISC for the next few years."

"A space prison for me! You must be kidding!"

McVeigh says, shocked and startled. "You mean I can't go back to earth, ever, with my new heart?"

"I wouldn't state that conclusively," Bergstrom hedges. "But you'd need weightlessness during the night. You could of course visit the earth every month for a few hours, I'm sure."

"But I'll have to be in this bed every night!" McVeigh throws a quick glance at the artificial heart. "I did a lot of thinking last night. Thoughts become mountainous in the dark, don't they? The bright ones become brighter and the dark ones darker."

Bergstrom takes off his coat and hangs it over his chair, a habit of his to assure patients that he is going to work, like a laborer. Pulling his chair close to the bed, he sits down and takes McVeigh's wrist to measure the painful beating of his pulse.

"I'd like to give you a shot of Coramine," he says casually.

"What for? I'm wired up, and if anything happens to me, that nurse at the telemeter controls will sound the fire alarm. No, Ingmar, I have things on my mind that I want to talk over with you. Coramine wouldn't help." For the first time he calls Bergstrom by his first name.

"I'll keep it a doctor's secret. Privileged information!"

"Not necessarily. But I don't think that piece of plastic would do me any good."

"No need to be afraid of the operation. There's a ninety percent chance of total recovery."

"Afraid? Ingmar, I just can't keep up with the world. Things keep changing so quickly—time is leaving me behind. I don't belong anywhere."

"What makes you say that?" Bergstrom asks.

"You'll understand me in a minute." McVeigh moves the cantilevered hospital table close and takes a sip from a glass tube. "First, there's Nicopulos' decision to free those spacejackers. Crime rewarded by a judge who supposedly represents that blindfolded lady with the scales."

"He had no choice," Bergstrom says evenly. "There are still people in the Space Prison; they threaten to blow it up. The debris would endanger the ISC. They won't do that as long as they know their friends are safe."

"I know, I know! Powers told me. He agreed with Nicopulos. Even that half-wit Mancini concurred. That woman, Vera Stern, holds all the trumps."

"What would you have proposed?"

"I'm no scientist. I can't quarrel with Nicopulos' decision because I know of no alternative. But what convinces me that I don't belong to this age is that Nicopulos and Powers don't believe in punishment for criminals. Well, I was brought up by a minister father and a religious mother. I sang in church. I swore on the Bible not once but twice when I became President. I found my answers in that book. But what does Nicopulos do with those fifty characters? Those who didn't kill each other off, they'll be working in control rooms, some in the kitchen, some in the hotel, some will even become security guards! Guzmán joins the legal department! Even that embezzler Svoboda becomes—what? A croupier in the casino! Because he likes to gamble! And what about Dubois, who's being paid by Ground and suddenly changes sides, defending the spacejackers? Mancini still keeps him on the payroll. Now what do you make of that?"

"You didn't mention Dr. Behrmann, who is joining my department," Bergstrom adds, noticing that McVeigh's pale cheeks are taking on a healthy color. "He's an excellent diagnostician. He might even look after you!"

"Great! That man is a radical. He was sent up for life, for trying to overthrow his government. Now he's not only reprieved, but being rewarded!"

"He might have had his motives." Bergstrom checks McVeigh's pulse, which is beating in an unhurried rhythm.

"Is there a motive for murder that excuses it?"

"Nicopulos believes that punishment rarely changes criminals. Making them responsible for things of value integrates them into society."

"That's what I'm talking about," McVeigh says in a flat voice. "How does he cope with that old blackmailing woman in the Space Prison? She tells him what to do. Nicopulos has an approach to lawlessness that I could never accept. Now, can you imagine what would happen if I became the head of the ISC and had to second Nicopulos in his decisions? I couldn't. I wouldn't. Having an atomic heart to keep me living for a hundred years would turn me into a robot. Just staying alive is no incentive for me, Ingmar. Being marooned up here for eternity!" He shudders as if attacked by a sudden chill. "I don't intend to live like a fetus in a bottle."

"Are you saying you don't want to go through with the transplant?" Bergstrom asks.

"Exactly," says McVeigh. "The world changes too rapidly for me. And to know that I couldn't even escape into dying would be constant agony. No! That'd be like lying alive in my coffin!"

"You want to postpone the operation?" Bergstrom asks gravely. "You could do it any time you change your mind."

"I don't think that'll ever happen," McVeigh says, and there is peaceful resignation in his voice. "I'm going to live out the span of life allotted to me by nature. And I don't want you to use your medicine man's tricks on me when my hour has come."

# XXXIII

The *Spidery Dragon*, the spacecraft XC-17, floats in its test run.

"All systems working satisfactorily," says a dry voice from earth. Frazer in Menlo Park, Mandez in Punta Arenas, Rimsky in Tashkent, the tracking stations in Vevey, Goldstone and Tokyo form a net of spying eyes around the world, checking every function of the satellite whose destination will be the planet Mercury.

Lee looks through the Vycor window. The sun is above him, earth below.

The command module is pleasantly furnished with a desk, a couch, a library of books on microfilm to be projected on a small screen, the comforts of a home. To live in space is, for Lee, like living in his chalet in Thun.

Almost.

The video blinks. Lee switches on its vision. Tomlinson's kind face covers the screen.

"Still interested in being a space jockey?" Tomlinson asks without preliminaries.

"Of course. It's mystic," Lee replies.

"What makes you a mystic is the fear of being swallowed up in mysticism," Tomlinson says.

"Here we go again." Lee sighs. "A profound statement that doesn't mean anything."

"You can't arrive at the truth by using scientific methods."

"Knowledge, Jerry, not truth, is what science is about," Lee answers. There is an ease in their conversation, but both men are skirting a decision which will redirect Lee's life.

"Are you going to pilot the XC-Seventeen to Mercury and waste all that time?" Tomlinson asks.

"I haven't made up my mind."

The radio above Lee's head emits a melody, faintly at first, increasing in strength, a pleasant pealing of notes, old-fashioned in a three-quarter time like that of a nineteenth-century dance. The sound gains in volume, filling the tiny control room with its tune. The ten million cubic feet of the City in the Sky float past Lee's window. Astrocommuters and astrotugs scurry toward it, the hangar's iris opens, spitting out a ferry which rushes toward earth.

"You got a letter in the last mail," Tomlinson says, holding up an envelope. "Mauve. Scented." He looks meaningfully at Lee.

"That's twentieth-century stuff!" Lee says, but in his mind he sees Susanne's dark eyes, remembers how lithely she moved. "You're trying to catch me with old-fashioned tricks!"

"Those tricks will never become old-fashioned. But the ISC will, and so will the XC-Seventeen. They'll end up in a museum or be scrapped." Tomlinson sniffs the letter provocatively. "Science won't give you any answer to yourself. But this letter might."

Lee watches the slowly rotating globe below, its continents and oceans obscured by clouds. A deep longing tugs at him.

"XC-Seventeen. Come in. Need exact position for checking," Vevey's impersonal voice comes through the speaker.

Lee can make out the Swiss Alps below. Blue dots embedded in a chain of mountains covered by eternal snow: the Lake of Geneva, the lakes of Brienz and Thun.

"I'll redock the XC-Seventeen at our next node over the Pacific," Lee says without looking at Tomlinson. "Test run completed. We never need to test anything twice, do we, Jerry?"

"Shall I read that letter to you?" Tomlinson asks

slyly. "I'll put my voice through the scrambler. Nobody on earth or in space will be able to listen in."

"No. I'll open it myself."

The chalet in Thun grows gigantic in Lee's mind. The universe diminishes to a frame, enclosing it.